KARLEEN BRADFORD

THE
SCARLET
CROSS

THE FOURTH BOOK OF THE CRUSADES

HarperTrophyCanada™
An imprint of HarperCollinsPublishersLtd

The Scarlet Cross
© 2006 by Karleen Bradford.
All rights reserved.

Published by HarperTrophyCanada™, an imprint of
HarperCollins Publishers Ltd

HarperTrophyCanada™ is a trademark of HarperCollins Publishers.

First edition

HarperCollins books may be purchased for educational, business, or sales
promotional use through our Special Markets Department.

HarperCollins Publishers Ltd
2 Bloor Street East, 20th Floor
Toronto, Ontario, Canada
M4W 1A8

www.harpercollins.ca

Library and Archives Canada Cataloguing in Publication

Bradford, Karleen
The scarlet cross / Karleen Bradford.
ISBN-13: 978-0-00-639345-0
ISBN-10: 0-00-639345-4

1. Children's Crusade, 1212—Juvenile fiction. I. Title.
PS8553.R217S33 2006   JC813'.54   C2005-905468-9

HC 9 8 7 6 5 4 3 2 1

Printed and bound in the United States
Set in Plantin

For my Uncle Cubby,
who is always there for me

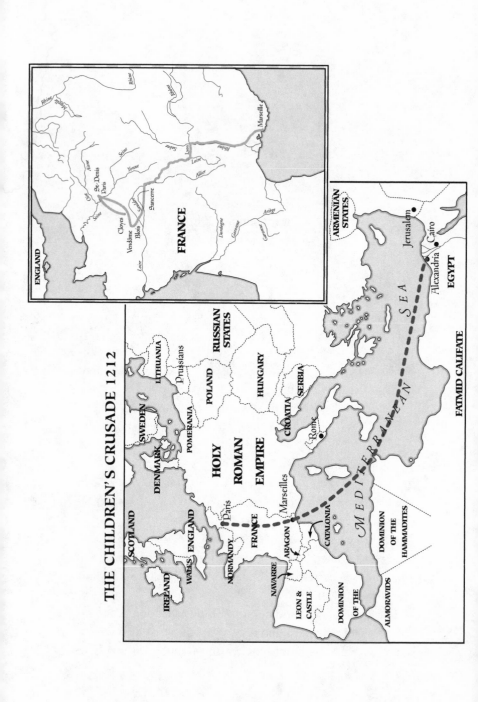

THE CHILDREN'S CRUSADE 1212

PROLOGUE

"God wills it!"

This was the cry of the crusaders that echoed throughout Europe and the Middle East for over four hundred years. The cry that inspired kings to abandon their kingdoms, knights to leave their families and holdings, priests and monks to desert their churches and abbeys, peasants to forsake their fields, and, finally, even children to run away from their fathers and mothers.

The crusading frenzy began in 1096, when Pope Urban II called for a quest to liberate Jerusalem from the Turkish Muslims. It was unthinkable to Christians at the time that Jerusalem could be as holy a city to those whom they considered to be heathen as it was to them. But probably not even the pope knew what obsession and fanaticism he was about to unleash.

The great princes and nobles of Europe responded to his call to take up the cross and restore Jerusalem to Christianity. They began to assemble their armies and make ready to journey to the Holy Land in the fall of that year, but Peter, a monk from Amiens, whom many called mad, could not wait. He preached crusade *now*. Peasants, priests, and minor nobles flocked to join him. The pope had promised pardon for their sins to all who went on crusade—the prisons of the Empire emptied out and thieves, rapists, and murderers swelled his ranks. Peter welcomed them all. This People's Crusade swept across Europe like a horde of ravening wolves, but made it no farther than the town of Civetot, in Turkey, where the Turkish forces swept down upon them and overwhelmed them.

The army that the pope had called for finally set out in September. In 1099, after almost three years of hardship and war, this first legitimate crusade succeeded in recapturing Jerusalem. The Christian kings of Jerusalem ruled for only eighty-eight years, however. In 1187, the great Muslim leader Salah-ud-Din, known to Christians as Saladin, retook the city.

A second crusade failed to reach Jerusalem. In 1192, a third crusade, led by King Richard Lionheart of England and King Philip of France, ended in a short-lived truce with Salah-ud-Din. A fourth crusade ended in disgrace with the sacking of Constantinople, a Christian city, in 1204.

By the year 1212, the crusading fervour had waned. In spite of the continuing zeal of the priests, people had become discouraged. The crusades had taken an enormous toll of men, women, and children. Homes and properties had been neglected or lost. People were turning more and more to their own affairs rather than venturing forth on what seemed an increasingly impossible war.

Then a shepherd boy, Stephen of Cloyes, had a vision in a field while tending his sheep. A man appeared to him, bearing a letter, which he bade Stephen take to King Philip of France. It was a missive commanding Stephen to raise an army of children to march on Jerusalem. These children were to accomplish what men had failed to do. By their faith alone, they would restore Jerusalem to Christendom. It was God's will, the mysterious stranger proclaimed.

Twenty thousand children answered Stephen's call, some as young as seven years old. He led them on a terrible journey across France to Marseilles. There, he believed, God would part the waters for them as he had for Moses, and they would walk through to the Holy Land.

CHAPTER ONE

The clang and clash of sword upon sword was deafening. War cries. Shouts of agony. Stephen could hear nothing else, see nothing but horses thundering toward him, their riders turbaned with brightly coloured robes flowing. He could feel the weight of his own weapon as he hefted it and swung once, and again, and yet again.

"God wills it!" he cried, and heard his own voice echoed ten times over by the multitude of mail-clad knights around him. He tossed a lock of hair out of his eyes. He surged forward . . .

Baa, baah.

Only a small part of his mind heard the frantic bleating.

Baah! Baah!

Impossible to ignore.

The noise and haze of battle died away. The knights faded into ghosts, the raging stallions disappeared. The sun shone brightly down onto a field studded with rocks and quietly nibbling sheep.

Stephen walked over to a steep-sided gully, looked down, and sighed. Not for him, the excitement of battle. Not for him, the honour of a knight fighting for the glory of God. It was the third time this week that this same ewe had managed to get into trouble. How the foolish sheep had managed to fall down there was a mystery; he could only hope she wasn't hurt.

All thoughts of glory and battle driven from his mind now, the sound tore at him. Each one of these sheep was precious to him. He had cared for them for most of his fifteen years—long enough that he knew their every quirk and eccentricity. He heaved another sigh. His sheep were not too astute and they were often stubborn. They could not see very well, either—probably one of the reasons why they got into so much trouble and then seemed incapable of getting out of it. But they were *his* sheep and he was responsible for them. There was nothing for it, he would have to climb down after this one.

"Hold your wailing, I'm coming!" he called to no effect. The ewe only intensified her cries.

He looked up at the darkening sky. Spring thunderclouds threatened; a flash of lightning lit up the field where he stood. It was late. He had left the rounding up of the flock much too long because of his daydreaming, but he could not help it. The village priests told such wondrous tales of the marvellous crusades to liberate the Holy Land from the heathen who occupied it that his mind was filled with the stories. The new, young priest, Father Martin, had even met a knight who had been part of King Philip's crusade, and he recounted the knight's exploits over and over every Sunday. The old priest, Father Jean-Paul, was as entranced with the tales as the rest of the village folk. At night Stephen dreamed of nothing else. His father and brother scoffed at him, of course.

5

"Only an idiot would leave a comfortable life to go traipsing off to the ends of the earth," his father said. He repeated it every time Stephen dared to bring up the subject.

Stephen shook his head to clear it. He was as simpleminded as his sheep. Time was passing, and he was sure of a beating from his father for bringing them back so late.

He started tentatively down into the gully, clasping bushes to keep from falling. One foot slipped out from under him and he tumbled. Bushes tore at him, stones gouged his hands and legs. By the time he came to a stop, one knee was scraped raw.

"*Par Dieu!*" he swore. It was one of his brother Gil's favourite oaths.

The ewe was stuck deep within a copse of furze. When she saw him she redoubled her bleating. Of course, she wasn't making the slightest effort to get herself out. Cursing yet again, Stephen plowed into the deceptively pretty, yellow-flowered bushes, and grasped the animal by an ear. He knew well the flowers hid thorns, and sure enough, one particularly vicious spine raked across his arm, drawing blood.

Now, even more terrified, the ewe bucked and kicked as Stephen got a better hold around her neck and pulled her out. The minute she was free she took off, leaping up the gully-side as nimbly as a goat. Stephen was left to clamber up behind her. By the time he reached the top, she was long gone to join the flock that was calling to her, and Stephen had used up every curse he had ever heard, and invented a few more. The village church bell called across the valley, tolling vespers as he made ready to herd his charges home.

It was dark by the time Stephen wended his way down from the pasture. His father and brother had long since returned from their work in the fields of Lord Belanger, the seigneur of their small village of Cloyes, to whom the villagers owed their feudal loyalty. Their work in his fields guaranteed them his protection and care, as well as providing them with a hut to live in.

Stephen herded his sheep into their pen for the night and latched the gate securely. A few chickens grumbled sleepily as he scuffed his way across the dirt yard. He paused by the door of his hut, listening. It was always wise to gauge what temper his father was in before entering.

As he strained to hear what might be going on inside, the door was flung open. His brother, Gil, burst out, almost knocking Stephen off his feet.

"Late you are, then," Gil growled. "You're in for a beating now, whelp." Without another word he strode off.

To the hostel, of course, Stephen thought bitterly. *My great lump of a brother does nothing but drink all night and work as little as possible, while I tend the sheep no matter how foul the weather. Yet it is me who my father beats, not him.* He knew why, but it did not help. His mother had died birthing him, and his father had never forgiven him for it. His father cursed the day he was born with every blow.

He tarried still, loath to go in, but his rumbling belly was not to be denied. He had taken only a crust of bread and a rind of hard cheese to eat that day. No matter that a beating was a certainty. If food was to be had afterwards, it would be worth it. He took a deep breath and stepped through the door that his brother had left ajar.

His father, Mattieu, sat at the table, red-faced and scowling. He was scooping up the last vestiges of a watery soup from his bowl with a crust of bread. He rose to his feet as Stephen entered.

"Where were you?" he growled. "Have I not told you the sheep must be penned before sunset? How many did you lose, you useless wretch?"

"None, Father," Stephen said. "I brought them all home safely. One did stray, but I found her. It was searching for her that made me late."

"And why did you lose her? Sleeping, I warrant."

"No, Father . . ." Stephen began, but Mattieu stepped forward and silenced him with a cuff on the ear.

For a moment anger rose hot within Stephen. He clenched his hand into a fist and drew back his arm before he could stop himself. Mattieu's face swam in front of his eyes.

"Strike me, would you?" Mattieu roared. "Strike *me!*" He snatched up a stick from the hearth.

Once, twice, three times he whipped Stephen. Across his shoulders, across his back. Stephen bowed his head and raised his hands to protect his face. When his father had finished, Stephen stood, shuddering, willing himself not to weep. He had not cried out. He would not give his father that satisfaction.

Mattieu glared at him a moment longer, then turned away. Beneath the pain, Stephen felt a small surge of triumph, but it was not until Mattieu had climbed the ladder into the loft above and thrown himself down to sleep that he dared help himself to food.

The fire had died down to a few smouldering embers. There was nothing but a cupful of the thin soup left in the pot, and that was cold as stone. Stephen gulped it down. He found a heel of barley bread and stuffed that into his mouth as well. A flagon of ale stood by the hearth, but he knew better than to drink that. His father would flay him alive if it were not there for the drinking in the morning. Instead, when he went outside to piss, he slaked his thirst with a drink from the stream that ran behind their hut.

He was ashamed of himself for giving in to his anger. He was becoming as hot-tempered and stupid as his father and his brother. He scuffed his way back to their hut and crept into the darkness.

What would his life have been like if his mother had lived? He could not help but believe that it would have been better than this. He knelt to whisper his paternoster into the darkness, then stumbled over the words of the Ave Maria. He had never learned them properly. A mother's job, that was, to teach her children their prayers.

When he was finished, he rose to stoke the fire so that it would last the night, and curled up on the mat beside it to take advantage of the last lingering bit of warmth. Now, in the dark stillness of the night, he could let his thoughts wander again. In his mind, Stephen could see a procession of helmed knights riding off to war, sitting tall in their saddles, shields held before them, lances at the ready. He could hear the creaking of their leather saddles, the footfalls of the horses. He could smell the sweat of men and beasts. On every knight's shoulder blazed a scarlet cross. A cross as red as blood.

"God wills it," he muttered to himself as sleep overtook him.

Gil staggered in much later. Stephen heard his brother throw himself down on his pallet, but he did not open his eyes. It took but little to enrage Gil when he was drunk, and one beating a night was enough.

✦ ✦ ✦

The next morning Stephen rose as the church bell announced prime, the early morning prayers. Carefully, he stepped over Gil's snoring body. He snatched up another crust of barley bread and a round of cheese that was only slightly mouldy, then he opened the door and stepped out. It was early April, and the day was still fresh and heavy with dew. He followed the clucking of a hen and pulled back the branches of a bush to find a newly laid egg. A treasure! He cradled it, still warm in his hand, then carefully put it in the pouch that dangled from the rope at his waist. He would make a fire and cook it when he reached the field. A feast, it would be, with the bread and cheese.

He opened the pen and hustled the sheep out. They were stupid with sleep and he had to throw clods of mud at them to get them moving. A dog. That was what he should have. A dog would be a great help, but his father had cuffed him even harder when he had suggested getting one.

"A dog!" he had cried. "Do you think us so rich that we could afford to feed such a beast? No, you wastrel. Tending the sheep is your job. Do not try to squirm out of it."

Stephen had known better than to argue. Still, a dog would have helped. He would gladly have shared his own food with it. Perhaps he would not daydream so much if he had a dog to keep him company, to talk to during the long hours of the day.

He shrugged. It was not to be.

Several boys his own age passed by him, hoes and scythes over their shoulders. They would be on their way to the fields to work, but Stephen knew better than to call out a greeting to them. Nor did they acknowledge him. Such was his father's reputation for meanness, and his brother's for bullying and thieving, that Stephen had never had any friends in the village. The tallest of the boys turned back. He was a lout named Yves, who had delighted in harassing Stephen ever since childhood.

"A chicken was missing from our henhouse this morning," he spat out. "And Pierre, here, saw your filthy brother hanging around our cottage after he left the tavern last night. You wouldn't be having chicken in your pot this evening, now would you?"

Stephen flushed, but before he could answer, the boy turned away. Stephen bit his lip until he tasted blood. The worst of it was that the accusation might be true. Not that he would have even a sniff of the bird if it were. Gil and his father would finish it off long before he returned. His father would never question where it came from, either. It had happened before.

Stephen threw another clod of mud at the sheep, a little too hard. It hit the lead sheep, the bellwether, on her flanks. She looked back over her shoulder and gave him a black look.

"My apologies, my maid," Stephen called out, then looked quickly after his tormentors. All he needed was for them to hear him apologizing to a sheep, but by great good fortune they were too far ahead by now.

✦ ✦ ✦

Stephen decided to take the sheep up to the high field this day. It was farther and a steep climb and the pasture was not as good, but this field inevitably drew him. Stories were told of a great battle that had taken place there between their own King Philip and the beast of England, King Richard, whom they called Lionheart. Once they had fought on the same side, those two great men, on one of the crusades that had failed to reclaim the holy city of Jerusalem for Christianity. But then, only a few years before Stephen had been born, they had fallen out and fought against each other in this very place.

The grass was littered with helms that were battered beyond use, bent and twisted pieces of swords, broken lances, bits of rusted chain mail. And bones, too. Bones of horses. Bones of men. Stephen could almost imagine the scarlet flowers that bloomed in and around them to be drops of blood. He had often felt the presence of ghosts around him in that field.

As he climbed, the sun warmed him. The sheep followed the bellwether on the narrow trail with hardly any urging on Stephen's part. The bell on the ewe's neck rang out with each step the animal took. The air here was clear and the sound was sharp and clean. Stephen's spirits began to lift. It was always thus when he climbed to these heights. He turned to look back. The village below seemed so small. Smoke curled from chimneys, here and there a tiny figure moved—to the stream to fetch water, to the church to hear Mass. From this distance it looked peaceful and safe.

He turned away and drew a deep breath. The sky was bright blue with the hint of summer in it. Only a few clouds scudded by. Beneath his feet some herb released a sharp, pungent smell.

His mother would have known the name for that herb, he thought. On the rare occasions when Mattieu spoke of her, he nearly always told how knowledgeable she had been about herbs.

"The village women came to her for their remedies," he said. "There was no illness she could not cure."

From his father's words and how he spoke, Stephen could almost believe that his father had not had such a temper before his mother's death. Certainly it seemed as if the women of the village had no fear of him then. And Gil, of course, would have been just a babe. It was hard for Stephen to think of his loutish brother as a small child, hanging onto his mother's skirts. Perhaps he had even been shy.

Would the family have been a happy one if he had not taken his mother's life? The thought laid guilt heavy upon him.

His father's temper had driven the village women away, and their daughters avoided Gil and looked at him with contempt. There was no place for Stephen's family in the village life now. There was no place for him.

He shrugged again. Such thoughts only led to sadness. He pushed them away and took another deep breath. Then he stooped to pick a sprig of the herb and tuck it in the rope around his waist.

When he reached the field the sun was high. The sheep scattered and began grazing. Something caught his eye. He bent to pick up a fragment of a sword. *Who had carried this?* he wondered. *What had been his fate?*

Only last Sunday, Father Martin had railed at the men in the congregation, accusing them of deserting God; of forgetting about His holy city.

"The crusades must begin again!" he had cried. "Jerusalem is still lost to us!"

Stephen had sat, letting the priest's words sink into him, fill him. *He* would not have forgotten. *He* would not have deserted God. Fighting for God must be the greatest act of faith a man could perform!

Now he closed his eyes and again, in his mind, the noise of battle rose around him.

And then a voice cut through his imaginings.

"Come here, Stephen," it said.

CHAPTER TWO⊙

Stephen spun around, shocked. For one terrified moment he thought that one of the ghosts that haunted this place had made itself visible to him. Then he realized that it was only a man. A man robed as if he were a priest, but not a priest that Stephen recognized from his village. Nor was his robe one that either of the priests of his church would wear. It was as torn and tattered as Stephen's own tunic. He had never seen the stranger before, he was certain of it. Why, then, did he seem familiar?

"Who are you?" he blurted out. "How do you know my name?"

"I am come from God, himself, Stephen, to call you to a holy mission."

Stephen stared at him, mouth agape. Had this man heard his very thoughts? He held Stephen's eyes with a fierce and piercing gaze.

"From...?" Stephen stammered. He could not pronounce the name of the Lord. Surely it would be blasphemy.

"From our Father," the man repeated. His voice was deep and sonorous. He towered over Stephen, seemed to grow taller even as he spoke.

Stephen could not help taking a step backwards. Still, the stranger's eyes held his own as surely as if there were a bond between them that could not be broken.

"I have a letter for you," the man said. "It commands you to lead an army of children to restore Jerusalem to the true faith. You have heard of Jerusalem, Stephen?"

"Of course," Stephen said, too terrified to move again. *Surely I should be running away from him,* he thought. *Surely he must be mad!* But the man's words held him spellbound.

"Where men have failed, you, Stephen, will conquer," the stranger said. His voice rose, he seemed to burn with energy. "Preach to the *young* people of France, summon them to follow you. Assemble a crusade of youths such as yourself, Stephen. Without weapons, by your faith alone, you will win our holiest of cities back for Christianity." He drew a rolled parchment from the folds of his robe and held it out. "Take this letter to King Philip of France," he ordered. "Tell him what I have said. He failed in his quest to win back Jerusalem, but he will help you. It is you, now, who will wage war for our Lord, Stephen." The stranger's voice grew even stronger. "And *you* will succeed! God wills it!" He echoed Stephen's own cry.

As if in a dream, Stephen tore his eyes away from the stranger's. As if in a dream, he saw his hand reach to take the letter.

Another dream—surely that was what this was!

And yet, the scroll that Stephen held in his hand felt real. He unrolled the coarse parchment and looked down at it. He was only a shepherd boy with no learning. He could not read it, but the marks spread across it in black ink jumped out and etched themselves into his brain.

Stephen looked up again. The man was gone. He whipped around, searching for him. There was no hiding place nearby. No one could have disappeared so quickly! He scanned the width and breadth of the field all around him. The sheep grazed peacefully, the bellwether's bell clanged as she moved to a fresh piece of pasture, and the herd moved with her, following her faithfully.

But of the stranger, there was no sign at all.

✦ ✦ ✦

Stephen sank down upon a stone. He held the missive in one hand, but away from him, almost fearfully. Did it really command him to lead a new crusade? To go to King Philip for help?

This could not be.

But what if it was?

What if God had heard his secret thoughts? Had answered his prayers? Miracles did happen—the priests told of them every Sunday. What if God were as angry as Father Martin at the apathy of men? Men had given up. Men had forgotten God's holy mission. Could it be that now the young, such as himself, were meant to fulfill His wishes?

Without weapons?

He looked down at the fragment of sword that he still held, then dropped it as if scalded. He rose to his feet. Stared unseeingly at the field around him. His head swam. Even if such a thing could be, why should he be chosen to lead? He was of no importance—never had been. There wasn't a soul in his village who deemed him of any worth at all, his father and brother included. In fact, they probably despised him more than did any of the others. Why would God choose *him*?

Suddenly his vision cleared and he saw the field through new eyes. Perhaps he had indeed been in the company, not of ghosts as he had thought, but of the Holy Spirit! Perhaps his dreams had not been dreams at all, but messages—prophecies!

He had to find out what the letter said. One of the village priests would be able to read it for him, but aside from his monthly confession, he had not actually spoken to either of them. On Sunday mornings he and his father came to hear Mass and then left. They never stayed to chat and laugh with the men and women of the village, much less talk to either Father Martin or Father Jean-Paul. What would they have had to say? And Gil, more often than not, did not even make it to Mass at all. He would have to take it to one of them, though. But not Father Jean-Paul. He might get nothing but a cuff on the ear for impertinence from the older priest. Father Martin seemed more likely. If the letter were nothing but a cruel hoax, the younger priest would be kinder, of that Stephen was certain.

With that decision, Stephen looked around for his sheep, finally aware of the fact that he hadn't heard the bellwether for some time. Sure enough, she had led the flock over a hillock and out of sight. Hastily gathering up his stick and his pack, Stephen tucked the parchment carefully into the pouch at his waist and set out after them.

For the rest of the day Stephen could think only of the stranger and his words. Every time he rested, he drew the letter out and looked at it again, staring at it almost as if he believed that this time he would be able to decipher it. So enthralled was he, that he entirely forgot to cook his egg. Indeed, he never even thought to make a fire. It was only when he went to put the parchment back in the pouch for what must have been the tenth time, that he felt wetness and realized the egg had cracked. Even that did not break the spell the stranger had cast upon him. He threw the shell away and cleaned the pouch with grass, then tucked the letter safe in the breast of his tunic. The rope around his waist that served as a belt would hold it there until he could clean the pouch better. He gnawed on the bread and cheese without even noticing the film of raw egg that clung to it.

The village bell started to peal nones, but Stephen paid no attention, so immersed was he in his thoughts. He was surprised when—it seemed but a few minutes later—it was announcing vespers and the sun was low in the sky. He would be late again tonight. Another beating awaited him for certain, but by the mercy of God, none of the sheep had strayed this day in spite of his inattention.

A beating he most certainly did receive, but Stephen hardly noticed it. He had returned in time to eat, but he gobbled up the thin soup without tasting it. When Gil asked a question, he did not hear. It was not until his brother cuffed him on the ear that Stephen awoke to the fact that somene had been speaking to him.

"What?" he stammered. "What say you?"

"Duller than dull you are, you clodpole!" Gil growled. "I asked where you took the sheep today, ninny."

"To . . . to the low pasture," Stephen lied. He did not want to tell the truth, afraid that if he did, Gil would some-how or other manage to tease the story of the mysterious stranger and the letter out of him. He did not want Gil to know of that. Nor did he want his father to find out.

Mattieu looked up briefly and grunted.

"No reason, then, for tarrying so long and coming back so late, boy. No reason at all."

"No, Father," Stephen answered quickly. "I'm sorry for it." Unconsciously, his hand strayed to the breast of his tunic. The crackle of the parchment concealed within reassured him.

It wasn't until Gil left for the hostel and his father lay snoring in the loft, that Stephen dared take the letter out and look at it again. He sat close to the hearthfire and held the parchment on his lap. By the dull light of the dying embers he could barely make out the writing on it. He traced the letters with a finger. If only he had the means to decipher the magic of them!

✦ ✦ ✦

Stephen must have fallen asleep with the letter still on his lap. He was awakened by a kick from his father. He had slept too long. Through their one small window he could see the first rays of dawn lightening the sky.

"Useless boy!" Mattieu growled. "You've nearly let the fire die out."

Letting the fire die was a great sin. It would take much work and effort with tinder and flint to light it again. Stephen jumped to his feet and grabbed for a bundle of sticks. He did not notice the parchment fall to the floor. As he coaxed the fire back to life, Gil, awakened by the noise, bent to pick up the missive.

"What's this?" he asked.

Mattieu was quick to snatch it out of Gil's hand. He stared at the parchment.

"Where did you get this, boy?" he demanded. "Where did you steal this from?"

"I didn't steal it, Father," Stephen protested, reaching out for the letter, almost in terror. How could he have been so careless?

"You must have," Mattieu replied. His face darkened. "None but the priests have writing such as this. Have you been stealing from the church?"

"No! I swear it!" Stephen cried. "It was given to me. By a man . . . ."

"What man? What man would give such a thing to you?" Mattieu roared. "You lie!" His eyes almost bulged from their sockets, so furious was he now.

"It is no lie. It is mine, give it back to me, Father, I beseech you," Stephen implored. "A man appeared to me in the field. He gave it to me. He said it was a message from God . . ."

Mattieu made the sign of the cross. Behind him, Gil did the same, his face horrified.

"And now you blaspheme! A message from God? Given to you? More like the work of the devil, I should think, and to the devil it shall return."

With one quick gesture he threw the parchment into the fire, which had blazed up again.

"NO!" Without thinking, Stephen thrust his hand into the flames. Despite the pain that shot through it, Stephen grasped the parchment, clasped it to his chest, and beat out the worm of fire that had begun to smoke along one edge of it.

"You dare!" Mattieu raised his arm and struck Stephen on the side of the head. It was by far the hardest blow he had ever given him.

Stephen stumbled. The room swam before his eyes. For a moment the fire and the smoke seemed to encircle him. He swayed, faint and dizzy, and almost fell, but the touch of the letter against his breast gave him strength. He drew himself up and shook his head to clear it. His father drew his arm back, readying himself for another blow, but Stephen leaped out of his reach.

"I do not lie!" he cried. "It *is* from God himself, and it is *you* who will go to the devil!" Then he turned, and before his stunned father could stop him, he pushed past Gil and ran out the door.

CHAPTER THREE

Stephen ran blindly away from his father's hut. He had no plan, no idea where he was going. He fumbled with the parchment and managed to tuck it back safely inside the breast of his tunic. His hand burned, and he held it close to his chest. In the brisk morning breeze it felt as if the flames were still licking at it.

He heard Mattieu's shout and turned his head to see him stumble out the door, but neither his father nor his brother gave chase. He rounded a bend and they were out of sight. *They could not catch me if they tried*, Stephen thought with grim satisfaction.

The sheep! Who would care for the sheep? Stephen came to a skidding halt. He could not abandon them. He almost turned to go back, but if he did that, his father would take the letter from him and destroy it. With Gil's help, which his brother would be only too glad to give, Stephen would not be able to stop him. This time the letter would burn for certain.

He took several great, gulping breaths of air. The church. That was the only place he could go now. To Father Martin. He fought down his guilt—he would have to leave the sheep to Gil. Stephen checked again to make certain that the letter was still safe, and then ran for the village.

A few women were already drawing water from the well as he crossed the village green. They looked at him curiously, then dropped their eyes. The church bell began to peal prime. Stephen stepped aside to allow a boy prodding a cow with a stick to pass him, then leaped to the other side of the path to avoid a flock of geese. He thought of his sheep again. They would be stirring, milling around in their pen. Anxious to be let out. The bellwether would be worried. Would Gil take them to pasture? Would Gil go after any that strayed?

He shook himself free of the thoughts, then followed some of the villagers into the gloomy, musty church and knelt in the darkest corner of the back. The church was small and poor. There were rustlings in the rushes on the floor—mice, perhaps rats, looking for crumbs. Stephen bowed his head to pray, but kept a wary eye out. The only light came from a small window near the front and the candles on the altar. Father Martin stood in front of the altar, assisting Father Jean-Paul as they prepared for the morning Mass. Stephen would have to wait for the opportunity to speak to him alone.

Stephen tried to catch his breath and slow his heart down. Surely it was beating so loudly that everyone in the church would hear it. Surely there was something so different about him this morning that they would all, with one accord, turn and stare at him.

But no one did. It was incredible to him, but not one of them took any notice of him at all. As far as the others in the church were concerned, it seemed as if it were a day just like any other. How could they not know that something earth-shattering had happened?

He stayed kneeling with eyes downcast, until the Mass was over and the villagers had left the church. Only when he was sure that the last one had left, did he dare to raise his eyes. Father Martin was tidying up the altar with his back to Stephen, Father Jean-Paul was nowhere to be seen. Stephen rose to his feet. He dusted off his knees. What should he do now? He took a hesitant step forward. He coughed.

Father Martin spun around.

"Goodness!" he exclaimed. "You startled me, boy."

Stephen could not find his voice. He stared dumbly at the priest.

"Do you want something?" Father Martin looked at him, puzzled.

"I . . ." Stephen began. "I have a letter. . . ."

"A letter?" Father Martin's eyebrows rose. He looked at Stephen more intently. "Stephen, is it not? The shepherd boy?"

"Yes," Stephen whispered, surprised that the priest knew his name.

"And you have a letter?" The priest's voice was incredulous now. "How is it that you have a letter, my son?"

"It was given to me . . . by a man. . . . Maybe not a man . . . . He said I must take it to the king. . . . I must . . ." Here Stephen's words failed him. Face flaming, he thrust his hand into the breast of his tunic and pulled out the scorched parchment. He was so overcome with embarrassment and fear that he did not even notice the pain in his hand. Father Martin saw the blisters, however, and drew in his breath.

"You have burned your hand sorely, my son," he said. "How did you so? Did you snatch that letter from a fire?"

"I did," Stephen said. Then, as he saw the priest frown, he cried out, "But I did not steal it. It was my letter! My father tried to burn it!"

Father Martin reached out and took Stephen by the shoulder.

"Come, Stephen, sit," he said. He drew Stephen down onto a rough bench beside him. "Now, tell me," he urged.

"I took my sheep to the high pasture yesterday," Stephen began. "I like it up there. A battle was fought there . . ." In his confusion and fear he began to babble. "I find things . . . bones . . . I found a piece of a sword yesterday. . . ."

"The letter," Father Martin interrupted him, staring at the parchment that Stephen clutched so tightly. "Tell me how you came by this letter."

Stephen drew a breath and got his tongue under control. "A man gave it to me," he gasped. "He appeared in the field beside me and gave it to me. And then he told me . . ." Stephen could not bring himself to repeat the words the man had spoken to him. He thrust out the parchment to the priest. "I cannot read it. Will you, Father, read it please?"

The priest took the letter from Stephen's trembling hand and held it up to the light coming in through the window. For several long moments he read, then he crossed himself.

"Do you know what this letter says, Stephen?" he asked finally. His voice shook as much as Stephen's.

"The man said it commanded me to lead an army," Stephen whispered. "To lead an army of young people like me. To do what older men have failed to do. To recapture our holy city of Jerusalem. He said I must take it to the king. It *cannot* say that, can it, Father?" The last words were more of a cry than a question.

"But it does, Stephen," Father Martin said. "That is exactly what it says." He fell to his knees. "Kneel with me, Stephen. We must pray."

Father Martin knelt for a long time, his head bowed. Beside him Stephen tried to pray, but his mind was too confused. He could not find the words. He found himself repeating instead, *Help me, oh Lord. Help me.*

Then the priest raised his head, opened his eyes, and fixed them on the altar.

"What did the man look like who gave you this letter, Stephen?" he asked.

Stephen looked up as well. His eyes met those of the Saviour who hung in his agony on the cross behind the altar.

"He looked like Him," he said.

Father Martin crossed himself and bowed his head again. Stephen could barely hear him whisper.

"Thank You, Lord. Thank You. You have answered my prayers."

✦ ✦ ✦

When he had finished praying, Father Martin rose to his feet.

"Follow me, Stephen," he said.

He led the boy to a small room at the back of the church. A straw pallet was piled in one corner and Stephen realized that this must be the priest's own room. He motioned to Stephen to sit on a low, three-legged stool, then reached to take down a pot from a shelf on the wall. His hands still trembled so that he almost dropped the pot as he untied the cloth fastened over its mouth. Then he dipped his fingers in and took Stephen's burned hand in his own. He began to smear ointment over the burns. Stephen felt the salve cooling and soothing the pain.

"We must go and speak to your father, Stephen," the priest said as he reached for a cloth to bind the hand. "We must seek his permission for you to leave."

"Leave?" Stephen echoed stupidly.

"Yes, leave. You must do as you have been bid. You must take your letter to the king."

"But how?" Stephen cried, suddenly terrified. The reality of what he was being asked to do had finally sunk in. "I know not how to find the king of France! And how could I speak to him? I would not be allowed!"

"The king is in Paris," Father Martin replied. "I will take you there." His mouth was set and his eyes were shining. "But first we must secure your father's permission," he added.

"That he will never give!" Stephen exclaimed. "He will beat me. He will burn the letter. He believes it to be the work of the devil!"

Father Martin paled. "It is *not* the work of the devil, Stephen," he said. "It is God's will. Your father will not dare to go against the will of God. Come. We will go there now."

He finished tying the bandage around Stephen's hand and motioned for him to follow. Stephen obeyed, but lagged behind. This priest did not know his father. Did not have experience with his temper. He fell even farther behind as Father Martin strode down the lane to the hut that Stephen had called home all his life.

"Maître Mattieu," the priest called. "Will you come out?"

Stephen's father appeared in the doorway. He had not yet left to work in the fields. His face flushed with anger when he saw his son. Stephen cast a quick glance at the sheep pen. It was empty. Gil must have taken the flock to pasture after all.

"What is this?" Stephen's father demanded. "Have you brought my wretched son home to me, then? Was it from you he stole that letter? Never fear, I'll beat him well for it!" He made as if to grab Stephen by the arm.

Father Martin forestalled him. The priest held out the parchment, but Stephen was glad to see that he kept good hold of it. "Did your son not tell you what this missive contains?" he asked. Before Mattieu could answer, the priest continued. "Did he not tell you that he has been chosen by our Lord to do what grown men have failed to accomplish?"

Mattieu stared at Father Martin, arm frozen in mid-air and mouth open wide in astonishment.

"Your son has been commanded to lead a crusade of young people to the Holy Land, to rescue Jerusalem from the infidels," Father Martin went on. "With Lord Belanger's permission, I will accompany him to the king, as he has been bade. We seek your permission, also, to let him go."

The priest's words came out stiff and awkward. He held himself rigid, as if anticipating Mattieu's fury, but in his face there was a grim determination.

At this, Mattieu seemed to come to his senses.

"God's will? My brat of a son? To the king?" His eyebrows shot up in shock. "What blabbering nonsense is this? The boy is a shepherd and a poor one at that. He has left his sheep—his brother had to care for them today. What has he to do with kings or crusades?"

Again he reached for Stephen, but Stephen slipped out of reach behind the priest.

Father Martin's voice grew cold. "It is God's will, Maître Mattieu. Would you disobey God?"

"You have lost your mind!" Mattieu bellowed. "My lump of a son chosen by God?" He lurched forward.

Stephen waited no longer. He turned and bolted back to the church and did not stop until he was in the dark safety of the building. Hardly had he time to catch his breath, when Father Martin appeared in the doorway.

"Wait here, Stephen," he said. He, too, was panting and out of breath. "Your father is an obstinate man, but he cannot thwart God's will. Our Lord's right to command you is greater by far than your father's. I must speak to Father Jean-Paul, and obtain permission from Lord Belanger to let us travel. Then I will put a few things together for us and we will be on our way." He disappeared again.

Stephen huddled in the church, expecting to hear his

father's roar at any moment. It seemed an eternity before
Father Martin reappeared.

"By great good fortune Lord Belanger's steward is with
Father Jean-Paul at this very moment," the young priest said.
"I showed them the letter and they would speak with you."

"Now?" Stephen stuttered. How could he face both the
old priest and Lord Belanger's steward?

"Of course, now," Father Martin replied. "And we must
make haste. We do not want your father trying to stop you.
Come along."

"But I cannot!" Stephen cried. "I cannot speak to such
important men!"

"Courage, my son," Father Martin replied. Then he
paused and studied Stephen thoughtfully. "You will need
far more courage than this, Stephen, if you embark on this
mission. If you do not think you possess it, then you must
give up now and go back to your sheep."

"But I have been commanded by God . . . !" Stephen
cried again.

"Then you must have faith that God will sustain you and
give you the strength you will need," Father Martin said.
He waited, his eyes fixed on Stephen's face.

Stephen stared back at him. He could not do it! It was
impossible!

And then it seemed as if the stranger were there in the
church with them; as if he were standing by Stephen's side.
"Where men have failed, you, Stephen, will conquer."

The man's words echoed in his mind, filled it to the
exclusion of everything else.

Wordlessly, he nodded and allowed Father Martin to
escort him out of the church, into Father Jean-Paul's hut.

The steward stood by the hearth, his legs braced wide
apart and his brow furrowed. Father Jean-Paul was sitting
by the window, Stephen's letter in his hand. As Stephen

and Father Martin entered, he looked up.

"Tell me, boy," the old priest said. "Tell me what has happened to you."

Stephen gulped. He tried to speak, then gulped again. Finally, the words came, and as he spoke, he felt the presence of the stranger once more.

When he finished there was silence. The steward looked at Father Jean-Paul.

"Do you believe this boy?" he asked.

Father Jean-Paul returned his gaze. "I do," he said. "I believe it is the sign we have been waiting for. The answer to all our prayers."

The steward turned to Stephen and Father Martin. "Then you have Lord Belanger's permission to leave," he said. For a moment he paused. "My father went on crusade," he added. "He died serving God in the Holy Land." For a moment there was a yearning in his eyes. "Go with God, boy," he said. "Would that I could go with you."

✦ ✦ ✦

Father Martin threw a bundle together with all possible speed. Then he turned to Stephen.

"You should carry this," he said, handing the letter back to him. "Guard it carefully."

Stephen made certain his pouch was clean enough now, then put the rolled parchment back into it.

They knelt for Father Jean-Paul's blessing, then Father Martin led Stephen quickly along the road that made its way out of the village. A road that Stephen had never before in his life trodden.

Stephen turned to take one last look at all he was leaving behind. Perhaps he would never see his village again. His father or his brother. He stared at the small patch of garden outside the church door. At the well in the centre of the village green. At the path that stretched back toward his hut. Though it had given him little comfort, he was leaving everything that was familiar to him—perhaps forever. Would he, too, die in the Holy Land as had the steward's father?

No. He was to triumph. The stranger had promised him that.

It is God's will, Stephen told himself desperately. *It* must *be*.

CHAPTER FOUR

Father Martin set a fast pace; Stephen had to stretch his long legs to keep up with him. He was bursting with questions, but he kept silent until the priest spoke.

"I know not how this thing has come to pass with you, Stephen," he said, "nor do I know how you are to accomplish what you have been commanded to do, but this I do know. God will show you the way. You must have faith."

"But why me?" Stephen burst out, unable to hold his tongue any longer. "I am nothing! A boy who tends sheep. Who would ever follow me? Who will believe me?"

"I believe you, to start with," Father Martin replied. "Have faith," he repeated.

Stephen fell silent again, but Father Martin's words did little to comfort him or to quell the chaos of his mind.

Stephen had been far too troubled that morning to think of food, but by midday he could no longer ignore the hunger pangs and rumbles in his empty belly. He was relieved when they reached a small stream and Father Martin paused by its banks. The priest threw down his bundle and knelt to drink.

"We will rest here, Stephen. I do not think your father will have followed us this far, if, indeed, he followed us at all. If he went to the church to complain, Father Jean-Paul will have sent him packing. The good father believes in you, even as I do. He has no tolerance for anyone who tries to thwart God's will."

"The letter is so powerful?" Stephen asked.

"It is."

"Could you read it to me?" Stephen begged. "I truly know not what it says."

Father Martin sat on the grass and undid his pack. "Sit, Stephen. We will share the bread and cheese that I have brought with me, then I will read it to you."

Stephen wrapped the chunk of cheese the priest gave him in a heel of bread and wolfed it down without tasting it. He slaked his thirst with the cool water from the stream, wiped his mouth with the back of his good hand, then settled down again beside the priest. Almost as if he were afraid to touch it, Stephen took the letter out of the pouch and handed it to Father Martin. The priest unrolled it slowly and began to read.

Hear now, God's word, all ye who read this!

This missive commands the shepherd boy, Stephen of Cloyes, to lead a crusade of the young to the Holy Land. He has been chosen by God to do what men have failed to accomplish. By the power of their faith alone, he and his followers shall confront the heathen and force them to acknowledge the One True God. He will restore Jerusalem to Christianity.

Stephen is charged to take this missive to King Philip of France. King Philip, in God's holy name, will help him with every means possible.

God wills it!

Father Martin handed the letter back to Stephen. Stephen stared at the markings on the parchment.

"But . . . ?" he began. "Who wrote this missive?" he asked. "I believe it came from God," he added quickly, as Father Martin's brows rose, "but surely a man must have fashioned the letters on the parchment? Surely God did not just cause them to be there?"

"Do you question our Lord's ability to do anything He chooses to do?" Father Martin asked, his brows furrowed now and his face stern.

"No," Stephen answered quickly. Too quickly, perhaps. "No, of course not, Father." But he was not satisfied.

The priest sighed. "God finds many ways to convey His commands, Stephen," he said. "It would not be impossible for Him to inspire some holy man to write down His words."

Stephen mulled the answer over in his head. It made sense to him. He could accept that.

"But . . . ?" he began again.

"More 'buts,' Stephen?" the priest asked.

"The man," Stephen stuttered. "The man who appeared to me. Who was he? Was it he who wrote the words?"

"Perhaps," Father Martin answered. "And perhaps he was not a man at all." He crossed himself. "It is not for you to question, Stephen. You have been commanded by God—you must obey. With faith. Without questions. Now, how long is it since you have made your confession?" he asked, briskly changing the subject.

Stephen knelt before the priest. He confessed to his usual sins of failure to respect his father, failure to pray as often as he should, failure to control his temper.

"And I left my sheep," he added. "I abandoned them." The thought of them still weighed heavily upon him. He did not confess to the terrible confusion in his mind. To the questions that still tormented him.

As they tidied up the remains of their simple meal and made ready to get on their way, Stephen heard the pealing of distant church bells.

Father Martin raised his head and looked in their direction. "I know the priest in that village," he said. "We will make our way there and he will give us shelter tonight. Tomorrow we will begin our journey."

But for Stephen, the journey had already begun.

✦ ✦ ✦

They came upon the village late that afternoon. To Stephen's eyes it seemed not much different from his own. A cluster of thatched huts straggled along the road leading into it. A village green nestled at its centre. Women here also filled jars at the well. Across the green a small stone church sat complacently in the sun. A few chickens scrabbled around its courtyard. Beside it was an enclosed space with weathered gravestones and tilted crosses. White flowers glistened on an early-flowering vine that climbed the fence and spilled over onto a low stone wall. Stephen could smell their fragrance, wafted over to him by an errant spring breeze.

Some boys of about his own age lounged against the wall. They watched Stephen and Father Martin curiously as the two approached. One of them, a tall, hulking boy who instantly reminded Stephen of Gil, raised his eyebrows and made a remark behind one hand to the others. They broke into smothered laughter. Father Martin took no notice of them.

"Stay here, Stephen," he said. "I will go in and talk with Father Pierre. I will call you when he is ready to speak with you."

Father Martin strode up the crumbling steps into the church. Stephen was left standing, at a loss as to what to do, when the taller boy shambled over to him and looked him up and down.

"A shepherd boy, that's what *you* look like," he said. "But not from around these parts. And what might you be doing here, then? Searching for your sheep?"

The words were not so rude, but the boy's manner was. Stephen bristled. His first thought was to tell the boy to mind his own affairs, then he remembered the letter now safely stowed in his pouch. Again he heard the voice of the stranger.

"*Preach to the young people of France, summon them to follow you.*"

It was God's will, he had said. God's will that he gather a band of young people such as himself to him, and here—here and now—he could begin! Stephen stood fast, gathered up his courage, and looked the boy in the eye.

"I *am* a shepherd," he said. "But *you* are my sheep."

A bad choice of words. The boy looked astounded, then angry.

"Sheep, do you call me?" he burst out. His face purpled and he looked even more like Gil.

Stephen realized his mistake. He hastened to explain.

"I am on a mission," he said. "I have been charged by God to lead a crusade to the Holy Land. You can be the first to join me! Come with me. We will be the ones to redeem Jerusalem for Christianity. This I have been promised!" In Stephen's enthusiasm, the words tumbled out so quickly, his tongue tripped over them.

The anger changed to a jeer. The boy turned to the others behind him and let out a whoop of laughter.

"It's not his sheep he's lost," he crowed. "It's his wits!"

"It is the truth!" Stephen cried. "You *must* believe me! I have been chosen by God!"

But at that the laughter turned to fury. The boy picked up a stone.

35

"Blasphemy!" he shouted. "You speak blasphemy!"

"Blasphemy!" another boy echoed, and then the cry was taken up by all of them.

The youth who held the stone threw it. It grazed Stephen's shoulder. The others were quick to join in, and stones rained down upon him. For an instant he stood frozen, then he ran for the sanctuary of the church.

Neither Father Martin nor Father Pierre was anywhere to be seen. Stephen fell to his knees before the altar, bruised and shaking. The boys did not dare to follow him. He had barely managed to bring himself under control when Father Martin entered through a low door in the back wall.

"What is the matter?" the priest asked, looking at Stephen with concern.

Stephen swiped at the blood that ran down his forehead and into his eyes. "I fell," he answered.

At that moment another priest entered the church through the same door. When he saw Stephen, he stopped short, then crossed himself.

"I am Father Pierre," he said. "You are welcome here, my son. Welcome to share my food and to take shelter here this night. Father Martin has told me of your holy visitation." He laid his hand on Stephen's shoulder in blessing.

This priest's acceptance of him and of his mission should have comforted Stephen, but it did not. That night he lay on the rushes of the church floor, wrapped in a woollen cloak that the good Father Pierre had procured for him. The priest had shared his evening meal with his two guests, and although it had been simple, the food had filled Stephen's belly. His body was satisfied, but not his mind. He had not been able to speak to Father Martin of what had happened with the village boys, but he could not stop thinking of it.

How could he possibly do God's bidding? What if it happened again? What if the young people of France would not listen to him? What if they greeted him everywhere with jeers and stones?

He tossed and turned; his hand throbbed with pain. Finally, he rose quietly to his feet, so as not to disturb Father Martin who snored beside him, and crept out of the church. In the moonlight he sat on the flower-strewn wall, inhaled again the scent. Surely, surely, God would not have set him on this mission if He had not thought that he could carry it out.

"You must obey," Father Martin had ordered him. "With faith. Without questions."

He had always said his prayers to the best of his abilities, accompanied his father to church on Sundays, and listened to the priests. Their holy words had comforted and inspired him. He had believed that he had faith, but did he? This was so far beyond anything that he could ever have imagined.

He sat there while the moon rose and while it descended again. A little before dawn he finally went back to his nest in the church. At last he slept, but his sleep was troubled by strange dreams. Voices called to him, some entreating, some commanding, but the message was always the same.

You, Stephen, you are the one. You will lead a crusade of innocents and you will deliver Jerusalem, the holiest of cities, back to us.

✦ ✦ ✦

Father Martin woke him the next morning as the church bell began to peal prime.

"We must make ready, Stephen," he said. "It will be good to be on the road early."

Stephen stared at him. The dawning of the sun did not

37

bring confidence. Instead, he was weary and troubled beyond the telling of it. His doubts and fears were magnified tenfold.

"I cannot do this, Father," he whispered. "Surely there is some mistake. It is knights and princes who go forth to battle, who wield swords and achieve glorious victories in God's name, not miserable shepherd boys like me. Not unarmed children!"

"There is no mistake, Stephen," Father Martin replied. "Of that I am certain. It is your own name that is inscribed in the letter. '*The shepherd boy, Stephen of Cloyes,*' it says. You, Stephen, are the chosen one. Our task now is to do as you were bade and show this letter to the king. He will tell us what to do next." The priest tidied up his pack and slung it over his shoulder with a flourish.

But despite Father Martin's eagerness and absolute conviction, his words only increased Stephen's dread. Show his letter to the king of France? Speak to him? Even if such a thing could come to pass, he was as terrified of that as he was of the whole quest.

CHAPTER FIVE

At first, because they were on the road so early, they saw no one else. They were accompanied only by the occasional bird and small animal scuttling in the woods through which they walked, but gradually the road became busier. Stephen found himself gawking at the passersby. It seemed that it was market day in the next town—a town that must certainly be bigger than Stephen's small village. Everything was new to him. Strange. Never before had he ventured so far from his home. He found himself walking closer and closer to Father Martin, for protection.

Carts rumbled by. Men and women carrying bundles joined the procession and trudged along with them—they called out cheery greetings and requests for blessings from the priest, which he was quick to give. Stephen was amazed at the ease with which Father Martin talked with these strangers; he himself was much too intimidated to join in. One man called out a ribald comment which set Stephen to blushing, but Father Martin did not appear shocked at all.

Stephen cast a quick glance up at the priest. How different he was today from what he was in church on a Sunday! He was so much more relaxed. So much more cheerful.

As the sun rose higher they overtook a man walking with a girl of about Stephen's own age, or perhaps slightly younger. The man was dirty and rough-looking. He walked with a scowl on his face, helping himself along with a stick. He carried a light pack, but the girl was bent under the weight of a bundle that was much too big and heavy for her. Her straw-coloured hair was tousled and fell in tangles over her face. When she reached to push a strand off her brow she looked up, straight at Stephen. Her eyes were grey, but so unexpectedly clear and penetrating that for a moment he was stunned.

Father Martin regarded the pair and his brows furrowed. Nevertheless he spoke civilly.

"Good morrow, sir," he said.

The lout did not respond with the usual respectful bob of his head, in fact he did not answer at all, merely scowling all the more fiercely.

"Your daughter labours under a heavy pack," Father Martin said. He slowed his pace to match theirs.

"She's not my daughter," the man fairly spat out. "My dead sister's whelp, and a useless wench at that." He glared at the girl and she flinched away from him, looking as if she expected to be beaten.

Stephen knew well that feeling. Before he realized what he was doing, he spoke.

"Let me carry that for you," he said to the girl. He reached to take the pack from her, but the man's stick cracked down on his arm with such force, that pain shot up to his shoulder.

"The boy meant only to help!" Father Martin exclaimed.

"We need no help from the likes of you," the fellow replied. "Begone with you and leave us alone."

Father Martin made as if to say something more, but the man raised his stick again.

"Begone, I said! Mind your own business, you black crow, you!"

Stephen drew in his breath. Never had he heard a priest spoken to in such fashion. Father Martin's mouth tightened. He seized Stephen's arm and pulled him away. Stephen glanced back over his shoulder. The girl was not looking after them; she walked with her eyes downcast. Father Martin strode on ahead of Stephen at a fast pace. Stephen had never seen him look so grim, but gradually the line of his mouth softened.

"How is your arm?" he asked. "That looked like a painful blow."

"Bruised, but nothing more," Stephen answered. "That man is a brute," he added.

"Pray for him," was all the priest would say. Privately, Stephen vowed no prayer for that oaf would ever pass his lips. He tried to put the memory of the girl's startling eyes out of his mind, but he could not. There had been a fierce defiance in her gaze, despite her bullying uncle. He rubbed at his arm with his burned hand—he could not tell which pained him more.

When they reached the town, they found themselves surrounded by a crowd of people. Stalls had been set up on the village green, and their owners were crying out and hawking their wares at the tops of their voices. Cattle lowed, dogs barked and fought, chickens cackled, and roosters crowed as if to usher in a thousand dawns. A myriad of smells overwhelmed Stephen—not all of them pleasant— but suddenly the scent of meat pies baking took precedence. Stephen felt the saliva come to his mouth and his stomach gave such a rumble that Father Martin heard it and laughed.

"I am hungry, too, my son, but we must go to the church first. I would talk with the priest here and tell him of your mission; beg his aid. Then we will purchase something to eat."

"But I have no coins," Stephen began.

"I have a few," Father Martin replied. "Later on we will most likely have to rely on the charity of the faithful, but for now we can buy one or two of those pies that are making your nose twitch and your belly growl." He smiled as he said this. His good humour had returned. Again, Stephen was surprised. Before now it had not occurred to him that priests could smile and laugh. Certainly old Father Jean-Paul never had. Father Martin's step was lighter now, too. He strode through the bustling marketplace, head high and nose sniffing as eagerly as Stephen's own. Truly, he seemed to be having a wonderful time.

The church sat on the other side of the green. Stephen hung back as they approached. Again, at the church doorstep, Father Martin bade him wait while he went in to find the priest. Again, a group of boys swarmed nearby, teasing the ever-present begging dogs. Stephen watched them warily. This time he would not try to enlist them. They would probably laugh and mock him as had the boys of the previous village. They might even stone him as well.

But if he were to do God's bidding, he must start somewhere . . . .

A hand on his shoulder startled him out of his thoughts. He jumped up to see Father Martin and an older, grey-haired priest beside him.

"This is Father Bertrand," Father Martin said. "He would speak with you."

Stephen followed the older priest into the dim interior of the empty church.

"Show him the letter, Stephen," Father Martin said. "Tell him what happened."

Stephen fumbled inside his pouch and brought out the letter. With downcast eyes and halting words, he repeated his story. Father Martin sat silently beside him. Father Bertrand asked more questions than either Father Martin or Father Jean-Paul had. He was more insistent, wanting Stephen to repeat even the smallest detail over and over. Finally, he seemed satisfied.

"Our Lord works in wondrous ways," he said. "Who would have thought He would have chosen an innocent such as you to do His work?"

"Suffer the little children to come unto me," Father Martin said quietly.

"Yes, so the Christ spoke," Father Bertrand agreed. He turned back to Stephen. "You will stay here this night. Tomorrow, after Mass, I will present you to the people of this town. I will tell them of your task and you will speak to them. You will begin here," he said.

+ + +

After returning to the market and filling their bellies to the bursting point with the meat pies that had tempted Stephen so, they returned to the church. Father Bertrand gave them blankets and told them they could shelter there for the night. This church was larger than the one in the last village and had pews on which Father Martin and Stephen could spread out their cloaks. But now, in the solemn darkness, Stephen could not sleep. Long after Father Martin's gentle snores began, he lay staring at the cross above the altar. The moon was high and a single beam struck in through one small window, illuminating the figure of Christ on the cross. Finally, Stephen cast off his covering and knelt in front of Him.

"Give me the words, oh, Lord," he prayed. "The words that will convince the people that I truly do Your will." But his heart felt as heavy as a stone and he shook with fear. The meat pies that he had devoured so eagerly had turned sour in his stomach. He could not get the memory of the boys who had jeered at him out of his mind. Nor of the man who had insulted Father Martin so. What if this was how they were to be received everywhere they went?

At this thought, the picture of the girl he had met on the way pushed itself back into his mind. He could see her looking at him still, with those clear, penetrating eyes. Finally, he slept.

✦ ✦ ✦

Stephen knelt all during Mass the next morning. His mind seethed with a tempest of thoughts and worries one moment, then turned terrifyingly blank the next. After the last blessing, Father Bertrand beckoned him. Stephen's heart plummeted and he felt suddenly sick. He had to force himself to make his way up to the priest, past all those assembled in the church. His legs trembled so that he feared they would give way beneath him. A hushed murmur arose as people craned their necks to get a better look at him.

"Who's this, then?" He heard the belligerent whisper and his heart sank even further, but Father Bertrand's voice quelled them.

"My people. My flock," he began. "You see before you a boy. A simple boy. Naught but a poor shepherd. But be not deceived by his appearance. This boy has been sent to us by our Lord God himself. He bears a letter for King Philip! A letter commanding him to lead a crusade of innocents to the Holy Land." The priest's voice rose. The words thundered out over the congregation. "Hear what he has to say. Listen to him. It is God's will!"

In the silence that followed his words, he turned to Stephen.

Stephen cleared his throat. He clenched his fists at his sides, willed his body to stop shaking. He had to speak. He reached into the pouch to feel the reassurance of the letter, then drew it out.

"This . . ." he began. To his horror, the word came out as a squeak. Someone in the congregation staring up at him laughed. Stephen cleared his throat again. What to say? How to say it?

Please, God, he prayed silently. *Please, God. Most merciful Father. I want to do as you commanded me, but I know not how. Help me! Give me the words!*

"This . . ." he began again. "This is not a missive given to me by human hands." His voice was still so weak that he was certain no one could hear him. He drew a deep breath and began yet again.

"This letter was given to me by the Christ himself!"

And with those words, came the belief, the certainty that this was true. All fear, all hesitation, vanished. He felt power thrilling into him—as though God were speaking through him. He straightened up to his full height and lifted his chin high. A lock of hair fell over his forehead. He tossed it back with a shake of his head and looked straight into the forest of eyes staring up at him.

"I come to speak to *you*, my brethren," he cried. "You who are young, like me. I come to call you to follow me. I am commanded to lead a new crusade to the Holy Land. Another crusade to restore our sacred city of Jerusalem to Christianity, but not, this time, a crusade of men armed with swords. Those men failed. This time it will be a crusade of young people such as you and I—armed only with our faith. And *we* will not fail. *Our* faith will be so strong that the heathen will surrender before it!"

Stephen looked out over the throng and saw that he had them in thrall. There was no more laughter. The young people in his audience fixed their gazes upon him without wavering. Their faces began to flush with enthusiasm as he spoke. He could see it happening!

"It is *we* who will accomplish what those men failed to do," he cried to them. "Follow me! Follow me and we will rescue Christendom itself! God wills it!"

Stephen knew not how much longer he spoke, but when he finished he was weak and empty, drenched in sweat. He would have fallen then, if the two priests had not taken him by the arms and led him out of the church into Father Bertrand's own sleeping quarters. There, they sat him down and gave him a cup of wine, and he drank it. It was the first wine Stephen had ever tasted, and the warmth of it sent strength coursing back through his body. Then he heard a hum of noise swelling rapidly.

"I have to go back," he said and struggled to his feet.

As soon as he reentered the church he was surrounded by the youths of the town. They clutched at his arms; they barraged him with questions. He could barely make himself heard above their voices. If some of the elders, the parents, were staring at him with stony, closed faces, he chose not to see them.

"Follow me," was all he could say. "Follow me and *we* will be the ones to return Jerusalem to the true faith. We *will* succeed where men have failed. I promise you."

And follow him some of them did. When he and Father Martin left town after a hasty midday meal, a small handful of boys came with them. Only a few. And only those without parents to hold them back. But it was a beginning.

CHAPTER SIX

They did not journey far that day. Father Martin had broken bread with Father Bertrand before they left, but Stephen had not been able to eat or even to think of food. By early afternoon, however, his appetite had returned and he was ravenous. Three of the boys who accompanied them were very young, certainly under ten years. They dogged his heels like adoring puppies and chattered non-stop. The fourth was a boy whom Stephen judged to be about his own age. This boy hung back, as if uncertain about the decision he had made, and walked silently with a scowl on his face.

"We will make camp for the night here," Father Martin said when they reached the banks of a small stream. Clear water burbled over rocks, tall trees cast a welcome shade.

"Come," the priest continued, throwing down his pack. "Let us gather wood and make a fire. Father Bertrand was most generous and I have the makings of a good soup here."

At this the younger boys' eyes brightened and they immediately set about searching for twigs and small branches.

The older boy threw himself down with his back to a tree, however, still scowling.

Stephen looked at him, annoyed. He was about to say something, when Father Martin touched his arm. The priest shook his head slightly.

"Give him a little time," he said.

Stephen shrugged and closed his mouth.

Father Martin soon had a good fire going. Stephen was surprised to see how adept the priest was at fire building. He fairly hopped around it. His robe swirled around his legs and, to Stephen's consternation, now and then almost brushed the flames. He seemed to be enjoying himself immensely.

"A fire brightens the spirit and the heart," he said, brushing ashes off his robe and rubbing his hands together over the heat. He pulled out a pot from his sack.

"You look strong, my lad," he called to the surly boy, "will you fill this for us?"

At first Stephen thought the boy would refuse, but then he lurched to his feet, gave a quick bob of his head to Father Martin, took the pot, and headed for the stream. When he returned with the pot full of water, Father Martin set it at the edge of the fire. He delved into his sack again and emerged with a handful of turnips and onions. These he cut up with a small knife that he took from a pocket in his cassock and tossed them into the water.

"And a final blessing!" he exclaimed as he pulled out a joint with shreds of meat still sticking to it. "God has provided us with a feast! Through Father Bertrand," he added hastily.

The smaller boys drew near to the fire. They watched eagerly as the water in the pot began to boil and the smell of vegetables and meat began to waft out of it. The smallest child licked his lips.

They look as if they have not eaten for days, Stephen thought. Hard upon that came another thought.

I am responsible for them now. I will have to provide for them.

That thought made him catch his breath.

Father Martin produced cheese and chunks of bread that were only slightly stale. When the soup was ready, they dipped the hard crusts into the soup and the bread softened up marvellously. The boys sopped up all the broth, then dipped in with their fingers to snatch out morsels of turnip and onions. For a while nothing was heard but slurping and grunts of satisfaction.

When they had finished, Father Martin took out the bone and wrapped it in a cloth.

"This will do us for many a meal," he said with a healthy burp. "Now," he said, "let us find out more about you lads."

There was a moment of silence, then the older boy spoke up.

"My name is Renard," he said. He wiped his mouth with the back of one hand, but his face still looked set and sullen in the firelight. "I have run away from a master who beats me day and night." He stared across the fire at Stephen. "I heard your words," he said. "I heard the promises you made." The tone of his voice was defiant and angry. "Is what you said true?" he demanded.

Stephen returned his look.

"I spoke the truth," he said. "I will keep the promises I made." He kept his voice steady, kept his eyes fixed onto Renard's, but with the coming of darkness, the fire that had filled him in the church when he preached was flickering. The certainty that had overwhelmed him began to crumble. It was as if the shadows of the night were entering his heart and chilling it. Could he really keep his vow to this boy? He looked again at the younger ones. The sense of responsibility flooded back over him tenfold. He could not desert them like he had deserted his sheep.

Father Martin broke in quickly, as if sensing Stephen's doubts.

"We will go to the king in Paris," he said. "King Philip will help us—Stephen's letter commands him to do so. He will provide us with the necessities for our journey. He cannot refuse us. It is God's will."

"The king?" the smallest boy asked, his voice hardly more than a whisper. "We are to see the king?"

"Stephen is," Father Martin answered in a firm voice. "It is God's will," he repeated. Then, less sternly, he asked, "What is your name, my child?"

"Dominic," the boy answered. He was a tiny urchin barely clothed in rags. His nose was runny and his face so dirty that it was unlikely it had ever known water. His hair hung in ratty strands down to his shoulders.

"How old are you?" the priest asked.

Dominic looked surprised. "I don't know, Father," he said. "However would I know that?"

"Did not your parents tell you?" Father Martin demanded.

"Truth, Father, I have no parents. Never have had."

Stephen looked at the child. It was not so surprising. Sickness had carried off many people. There were throngs of young orphans running wild in the towns and villages, living by their wits and the uncertain generosity of the folk—or by stealing.

One of the remaining two spoke up. "My name is Yves," he said.

"And I am Marc," the other put in. "We know how old we are. We are nine."

"We think," Yves added quickly.

More orphans, Stephen thought. But there was a spark about these two. A liveliness.

He took a good look at them. Almost as filthy as Dominic, but even so, he could see that their faces were identical.

Identical, too, were the dirty yellow curls that bushed out in halos around their heads. Both of their chins were greasy with fat from the soup. They were smiling broadly and their wide blue eyes shone.

Stephen almost smiled back, then his heart sank as he looked at the pitiful band clustered around the dying fire.

Children. They were, indeed, only children. And with such as these he was to conquer Jerusalem?

He gave his cloak to Dominic. Father Martin gave his to the twins, Yves and Marc. Renard had a torn blanket that he spread on the ground. They settled themselves to sleep.

The others were soon breathing deeply and evenly, but once again, sleep would not come to Stephen. He sat and stared into the fire while the stars appeared, one by one, and the moon rose from behind the trees. The fire died down and the moon shadows took over.

I cannot do this, he thought. *It is impossible. How could I ever have believed that God spoke through me?*

And then, out of the corner of his eye, Stephen saw something light dart between two trees. A shape, white against the darkness. He half rose, but the figure—if that was what it was—disappeared. He stared into the blackness until his eyes ached, but did not see it again.

A ghost? A spirit? Or an angel, perhaps, sent to watch over them?

It would be comforting to think that, but Stephen could not bring himself to do so. More likely just a trick of his imagination. He sighed, curled up, and finally slept.

✦ ✦ ✦

They awoke early the next morning. As Stephen rubbed his eyes, he heard Father Martin scrabbling around in his pouch.

"I know I saved a morsel of bread to break our fast," he complained. "It has vanished!"

"An animal, perhaps?" Stephen asked, not really paying the priest much mind. He knew the thieving ways of small animals in the forests and the fields.

"No, most certainly not. My pack has been opened and neatly tied up again," the priest insisted. "What kind of animal could do that?"

A human animal? The thought sprang into Stephen's mind. Had one of the boys stolen the bread? He looked at them, but all four lay sleeping still. Then a figure suddenly materialized out of the trees that surrounded them.

Stephen jumped to his feet, startled. As the figure grew nearer, to his astonishment he recognized the girl they had met going into town; the girl whose uncle had struck him on the arm. Unconsciously, even as he took a step toward her, he rubbed the sore spot.

The girl stood in the early-morning shadows and twisted her fingers in the folds of her shift. She held her head high—almost defiantly—and made no attempt to brush the strands of matted hair out of her eyes. The remarkable, clear grey eyes that he remembered so well. They stared at him now with the same piercing intensity.

Before Stephen could speak, she burst out.

"May I come with you?"

For a moment Stephen was taken aback. A maid? He had not considered that maidens would join his crusade as well.

"I am called Angeline," she added. She paused and took a deep breath. "I heard you speak. In the church. I have run away from my uncle. I hid in the trees and watched you last night, but I was afraid to show myself until now."

That explains the ghostlike figure, Stephen thought. *No angel, certainly.*

"I would go with you on your pilgrimage," the girl repeated.

Stephen found his voice. "The journey will be long," he began. "You are but a maid—"

"I am as strong as any boy," she shot back, suddenly angry.

Stephen stared at her. How could he refuse her? But there was no possible way she could accompany them. Beside him, Father Martin spoke up.

"This is not a journey for maidens," he said kindly. "Go back to your uncle, my child."

"I cannot!" she cried, the anger gone as quickly as it had surfaced. "He beats me. And I fear far worse than beatings at his hands. I beg you, let me join you. I have nowhere else to go!"

Stephen opened his mouth to echo Father Martin's command, but the words stuck in his throat. She looked so lost, so desperate. And those eyes of hers—they seemed to be drilling into his very soul.

Without willing it, without even consciously deciding to speak, he found himself saying, "Join us, then. Come with us."

Father Martin snorted. A sound of disapproval. He turned away.

"I'm sorry," Angeline cried to the priest's back. She dug into a pouch at her waist and came up with a crust of bread. "I stole your bread, Father. Forgive me—I was so hungry. This is what is left. Take it, please."

Father Martin turned around. He glowered at the girl.

"So that is what happened," he said. Then, as she held out the grey scrap of bread to him, his face softened.

"Keep the bread," he said. "There is nothing to forgive when a child steals out of hunger. I ask only that you share it with that little one there. He has a hunger as great as yours. Perhaps greater." He pointed to Dominic, who was sitting up now and surveying the scene, open-mouthed.

"I will!" Angeline said. "Thank you, Father." She sank to the ground beside Dominic and drew him close to her, then ripped the bread in half and popped his share into his gaping mouth.

For a moment the little boy just sat there, then with a gulp, he closed his mouth and began chewing.

"Hoy!"

The cry startled Stephen. He spun around. Yves and Marc were sitting up, staring at the small piece of bread left in Angeline's hand. Their two faces bore identical expressions of angry dismay.

"What about us?" they asked with one aggrieved voice.

Angeline looked at them, then shrugged. With a sigh of resignation, but also with a wry twitch of her lips that she could not hide, she broke the remaining morsel in half and gave a piece each to the twins. Stephen saw Renard watching them hungrily, but the youth said nothing.

✦ ✦ ✦

Dew lay heavy on the fields as they stomped out the remains of their fire and made ready to start on their journey. There was a chill in the air.

"You had best take this," Stephen said, and held out his cloak to Angeline, brushing bits of grass and pine needles off it as he did so.

"I need it not," Angeline said. The half smile she had favoured the children with had gone. "I will not be a burden to you. I can take care of myself."

"As you wish," Stephen replied shortly. If the maid were going to be so stubborn, what could he do?

The weather grew warmer as the sun rose in the sky, however, and soon he found that the cloak was more of a hindrance than an aid. It was bulky and awkward to carry, but too hot to wear. He and Father Martin led the way, Renard came next and, behind him, Angeline with the three younger ones. The children seemed to have deserted

Stephen for her. That did nothing to improve his humour. Was he not the leader here?

At first, Stephen and the priest set out at their usual pace, but they soon realized that the younger ones could not keep up. They were forced to slow down. Stephen fretted. In truth, he had no idea at all of how far the journey would be, but surely at this rate, it would take them much too long.

The road wound through the forest and then the trees began to thin out. They descended into a small valley where another village lay sleeping in the morning sun. The steeple of a stone church beckoned to them as if in welcome.

"We will break our fast here," Father Martin said. "Perhaps the priest of this village will give us food."

But it was not to be.

The priest came out to the village steps to greet them, but no sooner had he laid eyes on Stephen's letter and heard Father Martin's words, than he purpled with rage.

"What foolishness is this?" he cried. "What nonsense? Worse than nonsense! Children will set Jerusalem free? You have been misled by the devil himself!"

Drawn by the priest's angry outburst, a crowd began to assemble around them. Stephen tried to speak, but the villagers took their cue from their priest and drowned out his words with angry mutterings that grew louder and louder.

"Away with you!" the priest cried. "We will have no dealings with you. Do you think to do what grown men have not accomplished? You are sent by the devil to steal away our children—that is what you have come to do. Away with you! And shame on you," he berated Father Martin. "Shame on you for encouraging this misbegotten boy!"

The murmurings changed to shouts and angry catcalls. A stone flew out of the crowd and hit Dominic. Angeline cried out and ran to pick him up, then she turned and fled with him. Yves and Marc were quick to follow her, Renard slunk after them. Only Father Martin stood fast. Another stone grazed Stephen's shoulder. Just so had the boys of the other village stoned him. For a moment he despaired, and then a familiar fury rose within him. He would not submit to this humiliation again!

"God will punish you!" he cried to the mob surrounding them. "You have turned your backs on Him! You deny His will! You dare to throw stones at me and at God's own priest? He will punish you—each and every one of you. Wait and see. Just wait and see what He will do to you!"

A man poised to throw yet another stone paused, then dropped it. The shouting died away. Stephen stood fast, held his head high, and glared at the crowd.

Unable to meet Stephen's stare, one by one, the villagers began to disperse. The village priest gave a great *harrumph* of indignation, spread his hands wide as if disclaiming any part of the demonstration, and waddled back into his church. Finally, Stephen and Father Martin stood alone on the church steps. Only then did Stephen's rage subside enough for him to think clearly. Father Martin laid his arm across Stephen's shaking shoulders and led him through the village and out the other side of it. Shamefaced villagers moved out of their way to let them pass.

At the other side of the village Angeline waited with the three children. Renard hovered behind her, but Stephen had no desire to speak to them. They had abandoned him. At the first confrontation, they had fled.

"It was just one misguided priest," Father Martin began, but Stephen would not be comforted. He threw himself down on the ground and leaned against a tree trunk, head buried in his arms.

CHAPTER SEVEN

That night it rained. They made what shelter they could under the trees, but none of them slept, and by morning all were soaked through. Dominic coughed without ceasing.

"Do you still wish to come with us?" Stephen asked Angeline as he watched her trying vainly to wring the water out of her shift. He could not keep the irritation out of his voice.

"I do," she snapped back. "I am not so soft as you think."

Stephen shrugged. Were all maidens as mulish as she?

They set out fasting. What little food they had remaining they had shared the night before. There had been no way of making a fire, so they could not even boil water for a thin soup of roots and turnips. Stephen knew the others must be just as hungry as he, but there was nothing to be done for it. He could hardly bring himself to care in any case. The reception they had met with the day before still rankled. He cradled his hand close to his chest. It was healing, but it still burned. And his arm hurt as well. He rubbed it and cast a surreptitious glance at Angeline. She strode along beside him oblivious to the rain. She looked up and caught his eye. Without warning, she smiled. Caught by surprise, Stephen stared at her. Her whole face came alive when she smiled. By the time he thought to return the smile she had brushed a strand of wet hair off her forehead and turned back to walk with the younger boys.

The road soon became a sea of mud. It clung to their boots and sucked at their feet. After an hour, they were all exhausted with the effort of plowing through it.

Perhaps this will be the end of it, Stephen thought dispiritedly as he trudged on. *Perhaps this has been an impossible dream after all, and we will get no farther.* What would he do if he received the same welcome at the next village? Surely Father Martin would not expect him to carry on. But he couldn't go home. He could not bear the thought of facing his father after having left him in such defiance.

"What will you do if the priest in the next village refuses us help?"

Stephen was startled out of his thoughts by Renard, who had come up to walk beside him. The question echoed his own thoughts so exactly that at first he could not answer. Then he felt anger replacing despair. Who was this churlish boy to question him?

"We will face that when we come to it," Stephen said.

"I am hungry," Renard whined. "At least with my old master I was given food."

"Then return to him," Stephen barked and swiped angrily at the rain in his eyes.

Renard fell back to walk with Angeline. Stephen heard him say something to her, then heard her reply, which was equally as curt as his own.

"Instead of complaining, why do you not help one of these little ones," she said. "They can hardly walk in this muck."

At that, Renard tightened his lips and fell back even farther to walk with Father Martin. Either he did not dare voice his complaints to the priest or he had decided better of it, but Stephen heard no more from him.

The question still tormented Stephen, however. What *would* he do if they were turned out of the next village as well? Could he really abandon this quest—deny the will of God? *Was* it the will of God? Father Martin believed it to be so.

Stephen struggled with the turmoil in his mind, trying to make sense of it. Had he not yearned to fight for the glory of God? Had he not wished this above all other things? Could it not be that God had heard his prayers and this was his reward?

He set his mouth and strode ahead more firmly, ignoring the mud that clawed at his boots. He *had* been called by God. He *must* believe that, impossible as it seemed. He *had* to have faith. It was not for him to question—just to obey.

But it bothered Stephen that he had been so harsh with Renard. That was his father's way. It could not be his, if he were to follow God's word.

They paused for a rest when they heard church bells announcing sext, but did not bother to make a fire. The rain had ceased and the sun emerged from behind the clouds. The warmth was welcome, yet Father Martin would not let them tarry.

"The next village is nearby," he said. "Let us make for that." Then he added, "I will go ahead, Stephen. Perhaps if I speak with the village priest first, he might be more forthcoming."

Stephen was about to object—surely he should go with the priest—but at that moment Angeline called to him.

"Stephen, can you walk more slowly? We are having trouble here."

He looked back and saw her struggling to carry Dominic, who was still coughing. Yves and Marc trailed; Renard slouched far behind. Stephen took one last look at Father Martin, who was disappearing around a bend in the road, then shrugged and stopped to wait for Angeline to catch up to him. In spite of his resolve, he could not deny a small feeling of relief. Let Father Martin find out first what their welcome was to be. He reached out and took Dominic from Angeline.

"Ride pickaback on my shoulders," he said. Dominic brightened instantly and grabbed onto Stephen. He wound one arm around Stephen's neck and clasped him so tightly that Stephen began to choke.

"Take care!" Angeline cried, but she was laughing. "You are about to strangle Stephen! Do not hold him so tightly, child!"

Dominic loosened his hold, but then wound the other hand in Stephen's hair. Stephen let out a yelp of pain. Perhaps this was not such a good idea. He was about to drop the little boy back down into the mud, when Dominic let him go.

"I'm sorry," Dominic said. "Is this better?" He grasped Stephen by the shoulders.

"Much," Stephen gasped.

"My thanks," Angeline said. "That child is small, but carrying him is hard going in this mud."

"Giddy-up!" said Dominic.

Before Stephen could say anything, Angeline reached out and gave Dominic a shake.

"Push your luck no further," she admonished him. Her voice was stern, but her eyes, when they met Stephen's, were dancing.

What a contradiction of a maid! Stephen thought. He gave a hitch to settle Dominic better, then started off again. Yves and Marc skipped along beside him and Angeline.

"We are too big to be carried," Yves announced, but there was a small note of hope in his voice.

"Yes, aren't we?" asked Marc. There was even more hope in his voice. The two turned to look at Renard, who had caught them up. He only glared at them and hurried to walk ahead. The twins looked at each other and shrugged, then Yves snapped off a branch from a wayside bush and began to beat the air and stir up the mud with it. It wasn't long until he accidentally hit his brother. Marc was not hurt, but was splashed with mire. He then took a branch of his own, and the battle was on.

"Enough!" Angeline cried, and separated the two. She snatched both sticks out of their hands and threw them into the bushes. "If you want to travel with us, you must behave yourselves," she said. This time she was not smiling. Some of the mud had landed on her as well.

Stephen was surprised to see both boys acquiesce. They hung their heads and made a great show of walking obediently and quietly beside Angeline, but every once in a while one gave the other a sly push that was instantly returned.

Stephen shifted Dominic's weight to sit more comfortably. Ahead of him he could see smoke rising. How had Father Martin fared? he wondered. He could only hope Father Martin had managed to persuade this village priest to help them. They could not go another day without food.

+ + +

When they reached the village green, Stephen's heart sank. A crowd of people was gathered there. For a moment he faltered; he could not bring himself to face them. Then he made out Father Martin in the crowd standing beside an older priest. When these two caught sight of Stephen and his small band of followers, they made haste to greet him. Father Martin was beaming.

"Stephen," Father Martin called out. "You are welcome here! Father Benoit is anxious to meet you."

"Indeed I am, my son," the older priest said. "Come, refresh yourselves, all of you, and then you, Stephen, will tell me of this wondrous thing that has happened to you." He turned to the assembled villagers. "Let the boy eat and rest. I will bring him out to you at vespers. Now go about your business."

The villagers dispersed slowly, with many a curious glance at Stephen. One young boy hung back. He sat himself down on a low wall and it seemed as if he would wait there until Stephen returned.

Father Benoit led them into a small cottage close beside the church. There a woman tended a pot of soup that was simmering over the fire. The water rose to Stephen's mouth as he smelled it. To Stephen's surprise, the woman made a bob in his direction, then lowered her eyes quickly. It was as if she were in awe of him, but that could not be. He forgot the oddity as the priest settled them all around a long trestle table that took up most of the room.

No sooner had they seated themselves, than the woman brought bowls of steaming soup, a loaf of freshly baked bread, and a generous round of cheese. Dominic looked at the food on the table as if he had never seen such a feast before.

Most likely he hadn't, Stephen thought.

Even Yves and Marc were subdued, but that was probably because Angeline had them one on either side of her, Stephen noted. Only Renard began to slurp his soup noisily and reach for the bread before any words of blessing were said.

"Let us thank the Lord for this food," Father Martin said, an edge to his voice.

But once the grace was said, there was no holding back the famished boys. They finished up the soup and held their bowls out for more. The loaf of bread disappeared. Not even Angeline could restrain from gorging on the food.

When they had finished and not a morsel remained, Father Benoit settled himself back in his chair with a sigh and patted his abundant belly with satisfaction. He let out a great belch.

"Mistress Molly is a wondrous good cook," he said. "She takes excellent care of me."

True words, Stephen thought, *if we can judge by the looks of him.*

"Now," the priest said. "Show me this letter of yours, Stephen."

Stephen brought the letter out and handed it to Father Benoit. He watched warily as the priest read it.

"It is as your Father Martin told me," the priest said finally. He looked up at Stephen and crossed himself. "You are indeed chosen by God, my son."

To Stephen's astonishment, Father Benoit bowed his head to him. The priest looked up again. In his eyes was the same look of awe as had been in Mistress Molly's, and his words, when he spoke, were reverent.

"You must speak to our people," Father Benoit said. "We will give you shelter tonight and if some of our young ones want to join your crusade, they will go with the blessing of the church. It is a marvellous thing that you have been called to do." He rose to his feet, and again bowed his head to Stephen. "I must ring vespers now, and then you will speak."

The sun was setting as Stephen left Father Benoit's cottage and made his way back to the village green. There it seemed as if every soul who lived in the village was waiting to hear him. A buzz of anticipation greeted him. The boy Stephen had noticed before was still sitting on the wall.

Stephen could not get the picture of Father Benoit bowing his head to him out of his mind. A priest? A priest had paid him homage? Even so, he could not stop his legs from shaking. His mouth was suddenly dry. Could he find the words again? He looked to Father Martin for support, then, as his priest nodded reassuringly, he held the letter high with a trembling hand.

"One morning," he began. "One morning, while tending my sheep, I heard a voice call my name." A hush fell over the crowd. "I turned," Stephen said, "and a man stood before me. But he was not an ordinary man—he was the Christ himself!"

A murmur of astonishment rose from the crowd gathered around him. Stephen drank it in. He looked at the people staring up at him. Father Benoit knelt, and one by one, others fell to their knees as well. With that, all Stephen's doubts, all his fears, melted away. His hand that held the precious letter aloft steadied. Again, he felt the hot and burning power of God fill him and words poured out of him.

"The Christ himself!" he cried. He blazed with passion. "He gave me this letter! He told me it was a summons from God. A summons that commanded me to preach to the children of France. To summon them to follow me.

"'Assemble a crusade of children, Stephen,' He ordered me. 'Without weapons, by your faith alone, *you* will win our holiest of cities back for Christianity.'"

Stephen knew not for how long he preached but finally, once more, he was drained, with hardly strength enough to stand.

Father Martin was quick to take his arm. The villagers remained silent for a long moment, then a babble arose as they surged around him, but Stephen could speak no more. He allowed Father Martin to lead him back to Father Benoit's cottage. There a bed had been made for him close to the hearth.

"The others?" he managed to ask. "The boys? And Angeline?"

"They have been taken in by the townsfolk," the priest answered. "Fret not about them. They will be well taken care of."

✦ ✦ ✦

The next morning Stephen rose and broke his fast with the two priests after their prayers. When he left the cottage, Angeline, Renard, and the three younger children were waiting for him, along with several other boys. The villagers gathered to bid them farewell and pressed packets of bread and cheese on them. They took up their way again laden down with provisions.

"Did I not say it was only one misguided priest?" Father Martin exulted. He was sipping from a skin of wine Father Benoit had given him and grew merrier and merrier as the day went on. "Only one poor soul who could not see the will of the Lord. I'll wager you will not run up against another such as he during the remainder of our journey."

"Is Jerusalem very far then?" a voice asked from behind Stephen.

Stephen turned to see the boy who had been sitting on the wall. He was a scrawny young lad of about ten or eleven years of age, so Stephen guessed. He walked with a limp.

"What is your name?" Stephen asked.

"I don't have a name," the boy answered. "People just call me *le boiteux*. The cripple. Because of my leg. I cannot work much, so I beg for my food. But I want to go with you and I can walk," he hastened to add. "If it's not too far."

"It is not too far," Stephen answered. He felt light and full of confidence. Surely nothing was beyond him now. But as he spoke the words of encouragement to the boy he had a sudden twinge of uneasiness. How far *was* Jerusalem, really?

Not even Father Martin could tell him that.

CHAPTER EIGHT

"I talked long with Father Benoit last night," Father Martin said to Stephen as they sat by a lingering fire. They had made camp again in a woods. The villagers had been generous and there had been vegetables enough to make a thick soup. The newcomers had bolted it down gratefully and, their bellies full, now lay sleeping around the embers in the warm spring night. Only Angeline was still awake. She sat slightly apart from Stephen and Father Martin. Dominic was snuggled up against her as usual. The two imps, Yves and Marc, lay close together not far away.

Their faces looked so angelic in the flickering firelight, Stephen thought wryly, but those two were certainly not angels. They had been chased back to camp only that day by an irate villager who claimed he had caught them stealing turnips from his small garden.

"We have food enough," Stephen had protested when he chastised them. "There is no need for you to steal. Why did you do it?"

They had not answered him, merely hung their heads. He would have thought them contrite but for the sly smile he caught them exchanging.

"They know naught but stealing," Angeline had defended them.

"That is no excuse," Stephen had replied, stiffly. "We are on God's mission. We cannot accomplish that if we steal from the very people who would assist us."

"But that miserly man *wouldn't* give us anything," Marc exclaimed then, looking up with an aggrieved face. "We had to steal from him."

Now Stephen watched Angeline as she sat, staring into the fire. She looked as if her mind were far away; her face was sad.

What is she thinking about? he wondered. *Does she regret joining us?*

Then Father Martin interrupted his thoughts.

"Father Benoit told me that the king is holding court at his palace in St. Denys, just outside Paris, so that is where we should go," he said. "I gave him a letter that he kindly agreed to send to my brother, who is a priest in service to the bishop of Chartres. In it, I told my brother of you and of your mission. I asked him to persuade the bishop to recommend you to the king. You will have need of such a recommendation, I think, else the king might not agree to see you, and I am certain that my brother would be happy to help you obtain it. Even though many did not, my brother celebrated the truce that King Richard made with the Muslim Sultan Salah-ud-Din when he and King Philip went on crusade to the Holy Land. My brother has always been a peaceable man and he thought this a good solution—I know he feels it unfortunate that the truce did not last. He will be delighted to hear of your crusade, Stephen, and will do all in his power to help you."

Stephen's ponderings about Angeline fled from his mind. He looked up at the priest sharply. He had really only heard one thing.

"The king might refuse to see me?" he asked. "Even though I bear a letter from our Lord himself?" Truly, he had not thought that far ahead. He had been fearful about seeing the king, but he had not considered that the king would ignore a summons from God.

"We can but pray that he will," Father Martin replied.

The answer did not reassure Stephen. More doubts, now, to add to the misgivings that already weighed down his heart.

✦ ✦ ✦

The next morning, after they had broken their fast, Angeline came to sit beside him. She had a poultice of herbs wrapped in leaves.

"May I bind this around your arm?" she asked. "I can see that it is still horribly bruised from where my uncle struck you."

Stephen was at a loss for words. Angeline rushed on.

"I apologize for my clodpole of an uncle," she said. "He is naught but a brute. My mother taught me about herbs," she added quickly. "These will take away the swelling."

Stephen finally found his tongue.

"I thank you," he said. "It is not so painful . . ." Then, fearing that he seemed ungrateful, he added, "but I appreciate your poultice. It is kind of you."

Angeline smiled, and again Stephen was taken aback by the way her whole face brightened.

He sat and watched her while she bound the poultice onto his arm with a strip of cloth. Her fingers were quick and clever. The herbs felt cool and moist. Truly, they did ease the pain almost immediately.

"And your hand," Angeline said when she had finished.

"I see that Father Martin has tended to that. How did you burn it?"

"It is naught," Stephen replied. Too quickly. Too stiffly. He could not speak to her of his father.

Angeline drew back. "I am sorry," she said. "I did not mean to pry."

"No . . ." Stephen began. "It is not that . . ."

But Angeline had jumped to her feet and turned to chivvy the little ones into preparing to move on. Stephen bit his lip in frustration. It seemed he could not put two sentences together without offending this peppery young maid.

✦ ✦ ✦

It was impossible to remain glum that day, however. The sun shone with a warmth that promised summer and the air was filled with birdsong and the strong smell of earth awakening after a long and dismal winter. Stephen found himself striding along beside Father Martin with a spring in his step. He had not felt so eager and full of life since he had left his home. With full bellies for perhaps the first time in their lives, the three younger children cavorted around him and chattered without ceasing. Even Renard's scowl had faded. Then, behind him, he heard Angeline begin to sing. The three children immediately ran to trot beside her. This time Stephen felt no irritation, instead, he let himself relax and enjoy the sound of her voice.

She was singing about a wolf. "*Let's go for a walk in the woods,*" she sang, "*while the wolf is not there.*"

"Perhaps not the best of songs to be singing," Stephen muttered under his breath. "After all, there might well *be* wolves in the woods." But the three little ones loved it.

"*I'm coming!*" Angeline sang then in a deep, wolf-like voice. "*I'm coming to eat you!*" and the three screamed in mock terror and ran to Stephen for protection. He peeled them off his legs and furrowed his brow in warning at Angeline, but she laughed and kept on singing. By the time they had stopped for their midday rest, she had taught the children the words and they were happily playing parts—sometimes the wolf, sometimes the singer.

They came across a creek and Father Martin declared that they should stop there for their midday break. After they had eaten, they settled back to enjoy the sunshine. It was not long before Yves and Marc were sleeping. Renard dozed off as well, and even Father Martin, propped against a tree, began to snore. Stephen closed his eyes and leaned back against another tree. Bees buzzed in the tall grasses that lined the creek and a light breeze fingered through his hair. His mind drifted, at peace for the moment at least. Then Angeline's voice startled him.

"I am going to look for herbs to add to our pot tonight," she said. "Would you like to come with me?"

Stephen leaped to his feet.

"Most surely," he said. In his haste he tripped over a root and fell flat.

Par Dieu! he swore silently. What was it about this maid that caused him to be either irritated or clumsy?

Angeline smothered a laugh and bent to help him up. She held out her hand and he grasped it.

"*Shh,*" she whispered conspiratorially. "Let us not wake the others. The boys would be certain to want to come with us."

Stephen looked at the sleeping children. His followers they might be, and his responsibility, but it would be very restful to be away from them for a time.

"And truth to tell," Angeline added as she pulled him away from the campsite, "I am tired of Renard and his constant whining."

It would not be seemly to speak ill of one of his followers, Stephen thought, but privately he had to agree with her.

He watched as she bent and dug with a small knife and foraged amongst the bushes and grasses. She told him the names of the roots and herbs that she collected, but Stephen forgot them almost as soon as she named them. He contented himself with carrying the bundle for her.

After a while she sat down in the shade of a tall oak tree to rest. Stephen sat beside her and offered her his waterskin. She drank, then sighed deeply.

"I know not where this journey will end, Stephen," she said, "but I thank you for allowing me to join you. My life would have been a misery if I had been forced to stay with my uncle."

"Will you tell me about him?" Stephen said. "Why you were in his charge, and how you escaped him?"

Angeline frowned and bit her lip. "I do not even like to think upon him," she said, but after a moment she continued. "When my mother died," she said, "he came to claim all her possessions, meagre as they were. She had never spoken to me of him. I wonder not about that—he was a greedy man, a horrible man. We were on our way to the market in your village when you met us. I am sorry that he struck you and sorry that he insulted Father Martin."

"But how did you manage to get away from him?" Stephen asked.

"After selling all my poor mother's things at the market, he took a room at the hostel. He had the innkeeper lock me in a closet off the kitchen. I shivered there all night long, perched on a box to keep my feet out of the way of the rats. I knew I had to get away from him. He meant to take me back home with him and use me as a servant—and worse. When a kitchen maid opened the door by mistake the next morning, I knocked her down and ran for the church. I hid there, not knowing what else to do. I sat in a corner during Mass, then your priest introduced you, and I recognized you as the boy who had tried to help me the day before. I listened to you speak." She turned to look at Stephen.

"I had never heard words such as yours before. As you spoke, Stephen, I could *see* Jerusalem! Our village priest had talked often of the Holy Land, but never had he been able to awaken my mind to it as you did. I was frightened and knew not what I was going to do, but as I watched and listened to you, I felt that God had shown me a way out. I knew I had to go with you.

"I followed you when you left the village, taking care to keep out of your sight, and hid in the woods nearby while you slept. The rest of my story you know. It was my good fortune that you were at the church that day," she added.

"And mine, too, I think," Stephen said.

Angeline looked quickly at him, as if startled by his words.

Stephen was as astonished as she was by what he had said, but that night, when Dominic awoke from a nightmare whimpering that a wolf was about to eat him, he groaned and buried his head in his arms. Let Angeline take care of the child—it was her song.

✦ ✦ ✦

In the days that followed, Stephen regained his hope and his faith. He preached in every village and town along the way and at nearly every crossroads. The fields through which they passed were bright with young wheat and the air filled with the smoke of the burning tares—the weeds that farmers fought against constantly. Lambs gambolled in pastures, their tails flicking with excitement. Watching them brought a pang to Stephen's heart. He could not help wondering how his sheep were doing, but he closed his mind to the worry. His mission was much more important than a flock of sheep.

It did not rain again, and while that made for easier travelling, it was not good for the growing crops. The fields were dry and the farmers from the villages through which they passed complained about the lack of moisture.

Every time, after Stephen preached, more and more young people joined them. Not all were orphans or urchins. Some were children from good families, lured away from their parents by the spell of Stephen's voice. Nor were all of the parents in sympathy with the crusade, and sometimes an irate father would turn up in the evening to drag his unfortunate child away by the ear. More maidens joined, too. Now when Stephen looked back as they trudged on their way, he could not even count the number who followed them.

Numerous campfires sprang up every evening. The villagers and townsfolk continued to be generous and shared what they could with them. Most evenings they had bread and cheese aplenty and the pots that simmered over the fires were full of vegetables. Some of the boys were adept at snaring hares and other small animals, and when they did, those went into the pot as well. Angeline added herbs that she picked by the wayside. Finally, late in May, they reached the outskirts of St. Denys.

"This is a very holy city," Father Martin said as they approached it. Stephen walked on one side of the priest, Renard on the other.

"How so, Father?" Renard asked.

"It is named for St. Dionysius," Father Martin replied. "The Romans who ruled this land in his time had not yet received the true faith and they treated him cruelly. They tortured him for his beliefs and finally beheaded him. They threw his body into the River Seine, but he was such a holy man that he overcame death itself. To the horror of his murderers, he emerged again from the river, carrying his head in his hands all the way to this place, where he desired to be buried. Kings and queens and princes have been buried here ever since, and pilgrims come from all over France to worship at the shrines."

Renard's mouth dropped open in amazement. "He carried his own head so far?"

"To carry it so far would not be a wonder," Angeline said from behind them, "once he had managed that first step!" The words were accompanied by laughter.

Stephen whirled around.

"You should not speak so," he burst out before he could help himself.

"But the story is ridiculous," Angeline said.

Stephen scowled. Father Martin shook his head.

"Our Lord works His miracles in many ways," the priest said. His words were heavy with reproach. "Is not Stephen himself proof of that? You are young yet, Angeline," he added a little less sternly. "You will learn. If our Lord desired the good saint to walk from the river to this spot, He could make it happen."

Angeline raised an eyebrow, but she said no more and disappeared back into the crowd of children.

CHAPTER NINE

They entered St. Denys by the north gate and were immediately surrounded by a swarm of men and women, young and old. Stephen could not help gaping. Never had he seen such a large city and such huge numbers of people. There were vendors selling cheeses, bread, and flagons of wine. Pilgrims there were, too, with their wide-brimmed hats and their staves. A veritable babel of dialects and accents swirled around him. Beside him, Angeline was twisting and turning in circles as she walked in order to try to take everything in.

At the sight of the pilgrims, Stephen's heart rose. Here he would have fallow ground for his preaching, surely. But then a company of prelates galloped by, accompanied by an escort bearing shields and glittering swords. These churchmen looked rich and well fed. Stephen could see rings set with precious gemstones that caught the sunlight and winked on their fingers. As they rode carelessly through, Stephen's band was scattered to the sides of the path. Some of the horses nearly ran the children down. Angeline cried out indignantly.

Stephen's spirits sank again. Father Martin had told him that they must seek out the abbot of the Basilica of St. Denys in order to request an audience with the king. Father Martin hoped that the bishop of Chartres, at his brother's bidding, would have sent word to the abbot to prepare him for Stephen's arrival, but suppose the abbot was one of those puffed-up men? Suppose he thought himself far too important to meet with Stephen, let alone recommend him to the king?

When they reached the basilica, Stephen stared at it in awe. The walls of the church towered above them, with glorious windows of brilliantly coloured glass. It was crowned with spires that seemed to lift up to heaven. Stephen's steps faltered. This building was far too grand for him to even consider entering, but Father Martin strode forward and dragged him along by the arm. The priest's eyes were shining.

"Never," he breathed, "never did I think that I would see such a wonder!" He turned to Angeline and the ragtag band of children that crowded up behind her, mouths agape and eyes wide. Angeline was as overcome as any of them.

"Wait here," he commanded. The children, still stunned, seemed not to hear him. Finally, Angeline collected herself and led the younger ones to a grassy area around the church. The people hurrying by looked at them with curiosity, but no one approached them.

"I would come with you," Renard said, pushing through the crowd to stand by Stephen.

Father Martin frowned. "This is not your business, boy," he said curtly. "Wait here with the others." Still pulling Stephen along by the elbow, he made his way up the church steps and through the stone archway that led into the building.

Stephen looked back to see Renard staring after them with a sullen, mutinous glare.

Always, he is quick to push himself forward when he wants something, Stephen thought, *but rarely when there is work to do.* Then, mesmerized by the magnificence of the church, he forgot about Renard.

Inside, all was light—light broken into a myriad of rainbows by the coloured glass of the windows. The interior of the building was so big that several columns were needed to support the arched ceiling that soared far above them. The altar and cross were at the end of the nave, glowing in yet more shards of brilliantly hued light. Nothing could have been more different from the small, dark, heavy-walled churches of Cloyes and the villages through which they had passed. No Mass was being said at that time and the church was empty. Their footsteps echoed in the vast space.

A tall, formidable, grey-haired priest strode forward to greet them.

"The abbot, himself," Father Martin whispered. He bobbed his knee and bowed his head, then nudged Stephen to do the same. He spoke respectfully to the older man. "Good day, Father," he said. "I am Father Martin from the village of Cloyes."

The abbot stopped a short distance away from them. He fixed Stephen with a piercing gaze, as sharp as knives, then turned to Father Martin.

"So this is the boy I have been hearing about," he said.

"It is," Father Martin replied. He bobbed again.

"I have had word from the bishop of Chartres," the abbot said. "He told me of your coming and of this boy's petition to see the king."

Father Martin and Stephen exchanged a quick glance of relief.

"The king has agreed to grant the boy an audience in a few days' time."

It took a few seconds for Stephen to realize what he had said. It was done! He would see the king! But then the abbot continued and there was something in his voice that gave Stephen pause.

"You have a letter?" he asked, eyebrows raised. "A letter for the king?"

"I . . . I have," Stephen stuttered.

"You have it with you?" the abbot demanded.

"I do," Stephen answered. At another nudge from Father Martin he withdrew it from the pouch at his belt and held it out.

The abbot took it from him. He read it, his face expressionless. Then, to Stephen's dismay, he tucked it into the pocket of his robe.

"I will see that the king receives it," he said. His voice was cold. He turned and walked away.

Stephen and Father Martin stood for a moment, unsure as to what to do. Stephen looked to the priest, but before he could say anything, Father Martin shook his head.

"There is naught to be done," he said. His voice trembled a little. "He has promised that you will see the king. We must wait upon His Majesty's pleasure."

✦ ✦ ✦

Renard was waiting impatiently for them when they returned.

"Are you to see the king?" he asked as soon as Stephen reached him.

"Yes," Stephen replied.

"When?" Renard asked eagerly.

"I know not," Stephen answered. He could not shake off a feeling of foreboding. The abbott's demeanor had not been reassuring

The answer did not seem to satisfy Renard, but Stephen brushed by him impatiently and made his way to where Angeline was settling her brood of children.

I must be more charitable, Stephen thought as Renard gave way to him with a scowl, but the boy's surliness annoyed him. When he reached Angeline's side and she looked up at him with a bright smile, however, his heart gave a strange lurch and all thoughts of Renard fled from his mind.

"What news?" she asked.

"None yet," Stephen answered. "But there is hope, I think." He forced himself to put his fears aside. The abbot had said that the king would see him, after all. He must be patient. He threw himself down beside her and described his meeting with the abbot.

"He sounds like a frightening man," she said. "Do you believe that he will take your letter to the king?"

"I have to," Stephen answered.

Yves flew past them at that moment, hotly pursued by Marc. The two tumbled over Stephen's outstretched feet and were only saved from falling into the fire by Stephen and Angeline grabbing one each. Stephen looked up to meet her laughing eyes.

"These two are more trouble than they are worth!" Angeline exclaimed.

"That they are," Stephen agreed, arranging his features into a frown.

"What should we do with them?" she asked.

"Sell them in the next village," Stephen answered. "I hear villagers pay well for sturdy young lads."

"But they will work them to death," Angeline replied. She was keeping the edges of her mouth from turning up with an effort.

The two boys, suddenly very still, looked from one serious face to the other.

"Yes, that they will," Stephen replied. "But they would get a few years' hard labour out of them first."

"We'll behave!" Yves burst out.

"We will!" Marc echoed. "We promise!"

"Shall we give them one more chance?" Angeline asked Stephen.

He appeared to give the question deep thought. Two identical faces stared at him with mouths agape and eyes wide with fear.

"Well . . ." Stephen began. He had never seen the twins so quiet. "Perhaps . . ." he went on. Then he shrugged. "One more chance," he said, and loosed his hold on his boy. "But just one . . ." Before the words were out of his mouth, the child squirmed out of his grasp, Angeline released his twin, and the pair scampered away as quickly as they could.

Unable to control herself any longer, Angeline dissolved into laughter.

"I wonder how long they will be able to keep that pledge," she gasped.

"Not long, I warrant," Stephen answered with a wry twist to his lips. "A greater pair of scamps I have never met."

Nevertheless, his heart was filled with an unfamiliar warmth. A warmth that spread to his cheeks when Angeline moved closer to him and leaned her shoulder against his as she tossed another stick onto the fire.

✦ ✦ ✦

Father Martin said Mass the next morning as usual. When he finished, he turned to Stephen.

"Today," he said, "you will preach on the steps of the basilica itself."

"Will it be allowed?" Stephen asked.

"No order was given to forbid it," Father Martin replied.

Stephen was dubious. His stomach knotted with anxiety, but he followed Father Martin to the church door. There was no sign of the abbot. A few people were going in and out and others mingled near the bottom of the steps. Stephen placed himself on the top stair. He gave Father Martin a worried glance, but the priest only nodded encouragingly.

"My friends," Stephen began. His voice wavered. He was as nervous as he had been the very first time he had preached. No one seemed to be paying any attention to him.

"My friends," he called out again, loudly this time. "I am come here to deliver a message from God!"

At that, a few people turned toward him, their faces curious. Stephen took heart.

No matter how few listen, he thought, *I will preach to them.*

"A message commanding me to lead a crusade of children to Jerusalem!" he cried.

I have a letter, he was about to add, but even as he reached for the parchment he remembered that he had it no longer. For a moment his heart sank, then he steeled himself. It did not matter that he did not have the letter. He knew what it said.

"I was given a letter by the Christ," he cried again. "In that letter God commanded our king to help me. With his aid, I will lead a crusade of children to Jerusalem and succeed where men before us have failed. We, the children of France, will be the ones who restore Jerusalem to Christianity! I preach to you—to all the young people of this town. I call upon you to follow me! Follow me in Christ's name!"

Stephen felt his confidence returning with each word. As he spoke, more and more youths gathered at the foot of the steps, and that night a host of them joined Stephen's company. They crowded around him and besieged him with questions.

"Why must we free Jerusalem?" "Who stole Jerusalem from us?" "How?"

Stephen settled himself by the fire and signalled for silence. How little these children knew.

"Jerusalem was the city where our Christ was crucified," he began, choosing the words with care. "Where He died and was taken up to God. It is holy to us, but the infidels took it from us. Good Christian men have tried for many years to win it back, but they have failed. Now it is up to you . . ." he gestured to the throng surrounding him, "and to me."

"Why did the infidels want our city?" The question came out of the dark. It took Stephen by surprise. It was a question that he had never asked himself. He was at a loss for an answer.

"They worship their God there, too." Father Martin spoke for him.

"So Jerusalem is holy to them as well?"

Stephen looked quickly to see who had asked the questions, but he already knew. Angeline, of course.

✦ ✦ ✦

To Stephen's surprise, even older people joined as the days went by. He was taken aback one evening when he saw two men and a woman sitting by a fire on the edge of the field.

"What should we do?" he asked Father Martin.

The priest hesitated, then he answered. "Truly, what can we do? We cannot turn them away. If they have come in good faith, we must welcome them."

Stephen said no more, but he was troubled. The three were laughing and drinking wine. They did not look like devout pilgrims to him. As he watched, he saw Angeline making her way past them, back to the campsite. As usual, she was dogged by several small children. One of the men called out something to her that Stephen could not hear. Angeline snapped back a retort and shepherded the children quickly by.

"What did that man say to you?" Stephen asked, when she had settled herself by the fire and begun to make their evening soup.

"Naught that I would repeat," she answered, but her face was flushed and her eyes angry. "He reminded me of my uncle," she added.

✦ ✦ ✦

In the days that followed, while they waited upon the king's pleasure, Stephen preached every morning. His preaching grew stronger each day. The abbot did not reappear, but Stephen was more relieved than anything else about that. The man had intimidated him.

Then, on the night of the third day, Stephen had a dream. In his dream he saw a mighty sea stretching out before him, and as he watched, it parted. A path opened through it; the waters on either side of the path formed tall, glistening walls. In the far distance he could see a dome shining golden under a searing sun. He woke, puzzled, certain that this was a message from God, but he could not understand it. Nor could Father Martin give any explanation when he told him of it.

On the fourth morning, the abbot appeared just as Stephen was about to begin preaching. Stephen faltered. Was the abbot finally going to forbid him from preaching? But the abbot only looked at the waiting throng, which by now was considerable. His mouth settled into a grim line.

"The king will see you this morn," he said. Before Stephen had time to react, the abbot strode down the stairs and through the crowd that parted for him, even as the waters of the sea had parted for Stephen in his dream. With a startled glance at each other, Stephen and Father Martin made haste to follow him.

The abbot led the way down a tree-lined street, then turned a corner, and there in front of them was the palace. It was a massive building with turrets and high, crenellated walls. So huge was it that Stephen could not begin to take it all in. He stumbled as they mounted stairs that seemed to go on forever. He was sweating in the morning heat and he wiped his palms on his tunic.

At the top of the steps a footman barred their way, but at a word from the abbot, the man stood aside and they made their way into a great, echoing chamber. There, another man, dressed in crimson and gold robes that rustled with every step, appeared and bowed to the abbot.

"If you and the Father would wait here," he said. "I am to take the boy to His Majesty." He beckoned to Stephen and turned away.

Stephen cast one last anxious look at Father Martin, then followed.

They made their way through hall after hall, each more dazzling than the last. Stephen's senses swam with all the images of tapestries, gilded furniture, and candles blazing with light. He walked on carpets so soft that his feet in their ragged boots sank into them. He was so overcome that he could hardly breathe. Then the man stepped through yet another doorway and motioned Stephen in.

For a moment he could do nothing but gawk. The walls were whitewashed to an eye-blinding brightness and covered with the most richly embroidered of hangings. He could not help but reach out furtively and touch the one nearest him with a tentative finger. It was stiff with gold thread. The fleur-de-lys, King Philip's own emblem, hung from every pillar. Then he raised his eyes to the far end of the chamber and saw the king flanked by several footmen.

King Philip sat on a throne that was carved and embellished with gold. He was dressed in deep blue satin, a cape of shining silver draped over his shoulders. Beneath the golden crown that sparkled with jewels, his face looked grim and gaunt. Long, dark hair fell to his shoulders. Stephen stood staring, frozen, until a push from behind jolted him into movement.

"Go forward, boy, and kneel!" The words were harsh and commanding.

Another shove almost sent him sprawling. He made haste to approach the king and fell to his knees, his eyes lowered. All he could see, then, were two feet clad in grey boots of the softest, most supple leather. Ludicrously, he thought: *Those boots would not last a moment on the rocky fields where I tended my sheep.* Then he shook himself and looked up.

This close, the king was even more awe-inspiring. He stared down at Stephen with glittering eyes.

"You, boy. Stephen, I believe?"

"Yes, sire," Stephen answered. His voice quavered.

"I have been told of you and your wondrous tale," the king drawled, his eyebrows slightly lifted. "The bishop of Chartres implored me to grant you an audience."

To Stephen's relief, he saw that the king held his letter, but the tone of his voice did not bode well. The next words bore out his misgivings. The king waved the parchment at him.

"Do you really expect us to believe that our Lord has commanded you, a simple peasant boy, to lead a crusade to reclaim our holiest of cities? A crusade of *children*?" he demanded. "Do you really expect us to believe that the Christ himself gave you this letter?"

"I told the truth, sire. I did!" Stephen began to babble with dismay.

"We have no doubt that *you* believe this letter to be a missive from God. You are naught but a shepherd boy, easily deluded." His voice thundered over Stephen, furious now and the drawl gone. "But you have been deceived, my lad," he went on, the words falling on Stephen like rocks. "By some priest—perhaps well-meaning, perhaps not. This crusade of *children*—it is impossible. Do you really think that you can succeed where crusades led by mighty armies have failed? Where *we ourselves* failed?"

Stephen quailed before his anger, but then the king's voice softened, as if he felt some compassion for Stephen.

"Go home, boy," he said. "Go back to your sheep and leave the fighting to men who have been trained for it."

Stephen could not believe what he was hearing. It was impossible! He leaped to his feet.

"But it is the truth!" he cried. "It is truly God's will. I know it is!"

A footman stepped quickly forward and grasped his arm with a bruising grip.

"Back on your knees, boy!" he ordered and would have forced Stephen down, but the king raised his hand and forestalled him.

"He is but a poor, misguided lad. Leave him be." He looked at Stephen. "We know you believe what you say to be true, Stephen, but you must believe me that a crusade such as you propose could never succeed. You plan to walk to Jerusalem, with all your followers. You have no concept of how far that is. And you do not even know, do you, that a great sea lies between you and the Holy Land. How could you possibly cross that?"

At that, the meaning of Stephen's dream became clear.

"God will part the sea for me!" he cried. "As he did in the story of Moses!"

At this the king smiled, a tired, tolerant smile.

"Go home, Stephen," he repeated. "Cease this futile quest and return to the life our Lord meant for you."

"But I had a dream . . . !" Stephen began. "God promised me . . ."

The king gestured to one of the footmen. Before Stephen realized what was happening, he was hustled out of the great chamber, back down through the hallways, and out of the palace.

Father Martin and the abbot waited outside. When Father Martin saw Stephen's stricken face, his own visage paled. The abbot stood, impassive.

He knew all along what the king was going to say, Stephen thought bitterly.

"Begone, boy," the footman who had escorted him out said, and gave him one last push that all but sent him sprawling down the church steps.

"He would not hear me," Stephen managed to get out. "He would not believe me!"

The shock was such that he still could not make sense of what had happened. It had all been so quick!

How could the king refuse him? The letter had *promised* Stephen that the king would help him. At that thought Stephen felt his stomach give a lurch.

"My letter! He kept my letter!"

CHAPTER TEN

Stunned, Stephen walked back to where his followers waited. He did not notice when the abbot left them. Father Martin, beside him, was saying something, but Stephen could not make sense of the words.

Was this the end?

He stopped when he reached the encampment and looked around. Groups of children and young people covered the field; far too many now for him to know all of their names, but he did recognize the lame boy called *le boiteux* sitting slightly apart from the others. Makeshift shelters were set up here and there, but as the spring was warm and there had been no rain for several days, they were hardly needed. A few dogs scampered around, on the lookout for scraps. Campfires dotted the field. A hubbub of comfortable noise greeted him. Smells of cooking wafted through the air. Close by, he could see Angeline and Renard. Angeline had a pot boiling over a fire and was brewing up a soup. Yves and Marc were sniffing around it, Dominic as usual was close beside her. Several other youngsters tumbled in the grass around them. They were all laughing and cheerful as Angeline began to ladle the broth into bowls.

Could he tell them that their crusade was not to be? That, because of the words of their earthly king, their heavenly King's wishes were not to be carried out? As Stephen watched them, Renard caught sight of him and let out a cry. The boy ran toward him. Angeline looked up and smiled, her face alive with hope.

For a moment Stephen wanted nothing more than to turn and run. To hide somewhere. How could he face them? How could he tell them that their crusade was over before it had really begun? What would they do? They had all left whatever homes they had to follow him—would they be able to return? *He* certainly could not. Nor could Angeline and Renard go back to an uncle and a master from whom they had just escaped.

He had been the one who had preached to these young people; who had persuaded them to leave all they had ever known. Their lives rested in his hands. Was he to fail them now?

And then, just as the spirit of God filled him when he spoke to the people, he felt it fill him now. With resolve. With strength. He *would not* fail them. He *could not*! Above the basilica the oriflamme, the sacred and holy standard of France, snapped in the breeze. It shone red and gold, brave against the deep blue heaven. Here in this place where the saint had shown such determination, could he do no less?

He would go on! And he would take that very oriflamme as his banner! He straightened and threw back his head. He took a breath so deep that it drew pain.

I will do Your bidding, Lord, he vowed silently. *I need not the help of earthly kings. I need only my faith in You.*

"The king," Renard panted as he came up to where Stephen stood, "what did he say? Did he give us his blessing? Will he send an army to accompany us?"

"The king will not help us," Stephen replied.

Angeline had followed Renard and was just in time to hear Stephen's words.

"He will not help us?" she asked, aghast.

"No," Stephen said. "He dares to defy God's will out of arrogance. He will not believe that we could succeed where he failed, but we need him not. Look!" he commanded. He turned and gestured toward the multitude of people assembled in the field.

"Look at the army we have collected here," he cried. His voice rang out with passion. "This is but the beginning! We will gather *more* children to us. Many more! We will conquer the infidel on our own. We have our Heavenly Father's blessing, what need have we of an earthly king's!"

The village church bells began to peal sext. At that, Father Martin bent his head to Stephen's.

"Preach to them, Stephen," he urged, his voice as ardent as Stephen's. "Preach to your followers."

✦ ✦ ✦

Stephen would have moved on, but the next morning when he awoke it was to see people streaming into the field where they were encamped, even as the bells of the abbey began to peal the call to morning prayers.

"They believe," Father Martin exulted. "The people believe you!"

Stephen looked out over the growing crowd and his heart swelled with gratitude. This was the sign he had needed. He climbed a small knoll, turned to face the multitude. He tossed back the lock of hair that always fell in his eyes and raised his chin defiantly.

"My people," he began, and then he repeated the phrase, relishing the taste of the words in his mouth. "*My* people!" he cried.

✝ ✝ ✝

Stephen stayed in St. Denys for three more days. No one appeared to stop him so, defiantly, he preached on the steps of the basilica every morning and each day the numbers of his followers swelled. Children and young people flocked to him, as did more men and women and priests. A band of minstrels joined them to play and elevate their spirits. Not that their spirits needed elevating. With each passing day, Stephen grew stronger and more sure. He was invincible. He was God's vessel. Within *him* lived the truth and the spirit of the Lord.

Before they set out, he determined that they should all bear the emblem that crusaders before them had worn.

"A cross," he declared. "We shall each wear a cross of scarlet, as red as Christ's blood, on our shoulders, so that those who see us will know we are on God's mission."

That sent Angeline scurrying around the village, begging scraps of cloth, and she set to sewing.

Next, Stephen proclaimed that they should take the crusaders' oath. They must swear to follow him until they had accomplished their mission or die in the attempt. Humbly, the children lined up to kneel, one by one before him. Most of the men and women swore their oaths and sewed crosses on their shoulders, but in spite of Stephen's command, not all of them did so.

When everything was in readiness, they set off. Stephen sat enthroned in a cart filled with straw, drawn by a sturdy donkey, the gift of a sympathetic and wealthy farmer.

"The servant of the Lord should have a carriage," the man had said.

And when Stephen learned that Renard, whose old master had also been a farmer, knew how to manage the balky beast, he set him to driving it. Gone now was Renard's almost perpetual sullen scowl. He sat puffed with pride beside Stephen. He had even fashioned a canopy to protect Stephen and himself from the sun. Stephen had asked a local priest to obtain an oriflamme for him, and somehow or other, the priest had managed to do so. Now the flag waved proudly above him.

He beckoned to the leader of the minstrels.

"Go before us," he ordered. "Let us have music and merriment to lead us on our way!"

So the minstrels sang and capered along the path in front of him. One of the men plucked at the strings of a lyre, another played a flute and sometimes blew on a small, round clay whistle with holes in it that created a piercing tune. A third juggled balls in the air as he pranced along, and a fourth, a very short, very ugly man, tapped on a tambourine to keep them company. This last minstrel had a strange little creature that danced on a leash. It was the size of a dog, but it cavorted on its hind legs like a miniature man. It was covered in brown fur and had a small, worried face, beady little eyes, and ears that sat neatly close to its head. Stephen wondered to see it use its front paws almost as hands. Indeed, they looked more like hands than paws. When the juggler dropped a ball, the beast ran to retrieve it and handed it back to the man. Truly, the animal was a wonder.

The sun was bright, the air hot and buzzing with bees. The townsfolk turned out to speed them off and pressed last-minute gifts of food and wine upon them. Stephen stood tall in his cart as they left the town behind them, his hand resting on Renard's shoulder. His heart swelled with a pride that threatened to burst through his chest.

As the procession marched away from St. Denys and made its way toward Paris, Stephen sat down beside Renard. He turned to look over his shoulder at the line of people, young and old, stretching behind him. Father Martin walked by his side, having refused Stephen's offer to ride in the cart with him. Stephen saw Angeline farther on back and called to her.

"Come, Angeline, ride with us."

She looked up at him. She seemed angry, Stephen thought, but he could think of no reason why she should be. Was this not the most glorious of beginnings to their crusade?

"I have no intention of riding while all these little ones must walk," she snapped.

Stephen was taken aback. There was no need for such an attitude, surely. Then he had another thought.

"Find the boy who calls himself *le boiteux*, then," he said. "He would certainly like to ride with me."

"Too late for that," she retorted. "He did not come with us when we left St. Denys. He was fearful that he would not be able to keep up." With that she turned on her heel and melted back into the crowd.

Stephen was momentarily disconcerted, then he shrugged his shoulders. If Angeline was going to be so irritable, there was nothing he could do about it. But her behaviour created a small nugget of disappointment that spoiled somewhat the full glory of the day.

That night, when they assembled around their campfire, he saw that there were two more children hanging onto her skirts. A little girl who sniffled and wept and whose nose ran incessantly, and a young boy who looked to be no more than six years old.

She collects these children like fleas, Stephen thought.

The boy's face was smudged and dirty, and a large bruise welled across his forehead. He kept close to Angeline, but would not say a word to anyone, not even to her.

Yves and Marc made enough noise for all of them, however. After they had filled their bellies with soup and bread, they began to strut about, sticking out their scrawny chests to show off the crosses that Angeline had sewn on their ragged tunics. They had made swords out of sticks and were whacking at each other with them and crying out "God wills it!" with every blow. Stephen heaved a sigh of relief when the sound of the minstrels' music wafted over and the two rascals took themselves off to hear it.

The relief was short-lived, however. They ran back almost instantly with one of the men in hot pursuit.

"Stole the coins out of my hat, they did!" he cried.

Stephen reached out and caught one twin in each hand as they dashed by. He gave them a shake.

"Return them!" he bellowed.

Cowed for once, the two reluctantly opened their palms to display the coins. The man took them and shook an angry finger at the boys.

"If you play a trick like that again, you scurvy little scoundrels, I shall seek you out, hang you up to the nearest tree by your thumbs, and skin you like hares."

The two were quiet for almost the half of an hour after he left, then set to bashing each other with their swords again.

"Can you do naught with them?" Stephen demanded of Angeline.

"Naught," she answered shortly. "They have had to walk all day today—let them have their play."

"Thieving is not play," Stephen growled, then turned away, angry as well now. He threw himself down beside Father Martin. The priest, however, had his mind on other things.

"We must first make our way to Paris," he said. "A priest at the abbey told me that news of your crusade has gone ahead of you. Already children are gathered awaiting us. We can preach our crusade in Paris, then make our way back to Vendôme. That would be a good place to assemble and make ready to start the march south to Marseilles. What think you of that? The same priest was kind enough to draw me a map of the route we should take." He pulled a parchment out of the pocket of his robe.

Stephen stared at it, but the marks on it were as meaningless to him as his letter had been. Father Martin pointed to a cross at the top.

"There is Vendôme."

Stephen knew of Vendôme. It was not far from the village where the boys had stoned him. As he stared at the cross on the map, he could not help but nourish a small hope that the boys who had so mistreated him would hear of his crusade as he passed back along that way. Then they would know that he had spoken the truth. And it was close to his own village of Cloyes. Would his father hear the news? And his lout of a brother? What would they think? Would his father be proud of him, then? Would he forgive him for leaving home? When he returned in triumph from Jerusalem, his father would have to see that he had but followed God's will, and for once it would be he, not Gil, whom his father would praise . . . .

If he returned. He turned his mind away from that thought.

"Where is Marseilles?" he asked.

Father Martin pointed to the very bottom of the map. It seemed a long way from Vendôme. Beyond it the parchment was blank.

"Is that where we must cross the sea of which I dreamed?" Stephen asked.

"It is," Father Martin answered.

For a moment Stephen's heart sank, then he gave himself a shake.

"So be it," he said. "We will assemble at Vendôme."

CHAPTER ELEVEN

That night Stephen sat late by the dying fire after everyone else had rolled themselves up in their blankets and cloaks. He stared into the embers. In his mind's eye it seemed he could see the shapes of thousands of people in the flames that flickered and wove themselves around the burned wood. He could see crosses of blood-red scarlet flare up and then disappear into ashes. Unaccountably, even though it was a warm night and the fire still gave off a comfortable heat, he felt a chill shiver through him. He drew the cloak that Father Martin had given him closer and looked away.

How was he to do this thing? The question gnawed at him. So full of plans for the crusade, he had not let himself even think of how he was to conquer Jerusalem, but now, in the darkness, he could not suppress the question. He closed his eyes and tried to visualize himself striding through the gates of Jerusalem followed by hundreds, perhaps thousands of young people. They would be singing, the crosses on their shoulders would burn in the sun. But there his mind came to a halt and more questions surfaced. What would Jerusalem look like? Would the people welcome them? Who would he speak to? There was a sultan, Father Martin had told him. A kind of king. What if he treated Stephen in the same way that King Philip had? What if that king, too, turned him away? Angeline's words rose unbidden to his mind:

So Jerusalem is holy to them as well?

He pushed the words away. Jerusalem could not possibly be as holy to an infidel as it was to a Christian. Once he began to preach, the people would see the true way.

Faith. It always came back to that. He had to have faith that he was doing God's will. That God would show him the way. For now, all he could do was bury the questions and the doubts; preach to the children of France and lead them to Marseilles. Surely when God parted the waters for them, the course he must take would also be revealed to him.

The priest lay at his side, snoring softly. Beyond him, Angeline was curled up, surrounded by her little ones, for all the world like a mother cat with her kittens snuggled close around her. The sight brought back the memory of days and nights when he had nestled newborn orphan lambs to his chest to keep them warm.

For a moment he felt very alone. Who was caring for those lambs now? Had Gil learned how to tease the bellwether into going where he wished, not where she wanted? Stephen had been in charge of the sheep since he was seven years old and he knew their every whim. He could not believe Gil would be a good shepherd. He did not care enough.

As he watched, Angeline stirred in her sleep. She reached out with one hand and drew the child, Dominic, closer to her. Now, when there was no risk of her catching him at it, he let himself look long at her. He knew nothing of maidens. He did not understand how Angeline could be so caring one moment and so prickly the next. Nor did he understand what it was that he said or did that sometimes raised her hackles. And most of all, why it bothered him so much when she mocked him or was angry. She was only a maid. Why should her opinion be important to him when there were so many other things to worry about?

+ + +

The next morning, when they all awoke and began to make ready for the day, Stephen sat beside Angeline and shared his bread and cheese amongst her little ones. Almost, he could feel, they were like his lambs. Indeed, almost, they behaved as did the lambs. They butted into him, snatched the bread from his fingers, and then gambolled away to laugh and play. Watching them, Stephen could not help but laugh as well.

"It is time for morning Mass," Father Martin announced, standing and brushing crumbs from his robe.

Stephen jumped to his feet, then bent and held out a hand to Angeline. She took it, but instead of dropping it when she stood up, she held it for just the smallest speck of time longer. She was smiling as well, but looking at him quizzically.

"Do you know, Stephen," she said, "this is the first time I have seen you laugh!"

+ + +

That day they entered Paris. Never could Stephen have imagined such a city. As they drew near the walls he had to throw his head back farther and farther to look up at them.

"So high!" Renard said, his voice filled with wonder. But the marvels were only beginning.

They entered by the Porte St. Denys and the donkey's hooves clattered onto stones. The streets were paved over! Shops lined both sides of the narrow alley through which they made their way. Pigeons fluttered and flew from dovecotes on the roofs of the houses. Horses neighed and the rich smell of manure assaulted their noses from the stables tucked in beside the inns and hostels. There were people everywhere, shouting, calling, cursing—Stephen felt overwhelmed, almost smothered. The noise and the smells were overpowering. Paved or not, the streets still ran with offal and sewage. Stephen only had time to see Marc and Yves slopping into a filthy rivulet, then they ran out of sight.

"We must keep together," he shouted down to Father Martin, who was picking his way carefully alongside Stephen's cart and holding his robe high. He could not help noticing how scrawny the priest's bare ankles looked. How grimed with dirt his feet were in his battered boots.

Father Martin turned to look at the procession straggling behind them. His face was alight and his voice excited. "They will follow us," he called confidently back up to Stephen.

The procession was drawing stares and comments from the multitude through which they passed. Not all of the attention was friendly, however. It seemed that the horde of children invading the city was worrisome to many of the townsfolk.

"We are the children's crusade of God!" Stephen shouted out, but he was greeted only by open mouths and puzzled eyes.

No matter, he told himself. *They will listen when I preach.*

It was early afternoon. The church bells of the city began to peal nones. Father Martin was leading them now, fairly prancing in front of the cart. Stephen could only suppose that the priest from St. Denys had given him instructions as to where to go.

They passed a huge church in the process of being built. The air was filled with the dust from the stone that was being ground for it. A framework of wood enclosed the structure, reaching far up into the sky. Men were sawing wood, and carts loaded with supplies jostled Stephen's poor donkey cart as they forced their way by. Stephen could not believe how immense the building was. Huts clustered around the sides of it—the homes of those who laboured there by the looks of them.

"What is that building?" Stephen called to a passing man.

"The cathedral," the man shouted back. "The Cathedral of Notre Dame. It will be the wonder of France."

Stephen could well believe it.

The procession reached the banks of a great river.

"The River Seine," Father Martin turned back to announce. He was enjoying himself immensely.

Houses were set side by side on the bridge that crossed the river, their upper storeys almost joining those of the houses across from them so that it seemed as if they walked through a tunnel. Here also were the shops of goldsmiths and painters of miniature pictures. There were tables of money-changers, who were singing out what seemed to Stephen to be meaningless babel, but what he imagined must be information of the greatest importance, by the looks of the men and the serious mein of those who listened to them. Finally, as they reached the far side of the bridge, two monks made their way to Stephen's cart.

"Are you the boy chosen by God to lead a crusade to Jerusalem?" one asked.

Stephen, suddenly aware that his mouth was hanging open and that he was gawking, like the poorest of peasants, snapped his lips closed and drew himself up in his seat.

"I am," he said, and gestured to Renard to pull the donkey to a halt.

"We have been sent to guide you to our monastery," the other monk said. "We are Benedictine monks and there is room by our monastery for you to make camp."

"There are many, many children awaiting you here," the first monk put in. "Word has spread about the wondrous crusade that you lead." He crossed himself and bowed his head.

"Did I not tell you?" Father Martin crowed.

Stephen was still not used to a priest or monk bowing to *him*, but before he could say anything, the monk hurried on.

"There are nearly a hundred souls gathered at the orphanage of St. Jean le Rond as well, and more—oh, so many more—waiting in all the churches of Paris and the other monasteries. Truly, we have never seen such a sight!"

They bounded ahead, robes flying, and waved Stephen on to follow them with great sweeps of their arms. The crosses that hung on chains around their necks bobbed and swung with their exuberance. Father Martin hurried after them; Renard had to whip the donkey into a trot in order to keep up with them.

The monks led them outside the city through a farther gate onto the grounds of their monastery, which sat in a vast field. There was indeed room aplenty for them to make camp. Stephen ordered Renard to pull the cart up in the very middle of the field, then he jumped down. Children poured onto the field, chattering and dancing with excitement. The minstrels set up near Stephen and soon campfires were springing up as far around him as he could see. The multitude was so great that it took his breath away.

Monks and priests from the city began to arrive bearing food. Then the townsfolk came with food as well. There would be ample for all, Stephen saw with satisfaction. He remembered Angeline then, and looked around for her. At first he could see her nowhere, then, with relief, he saw her herding her small flock.

"Angeline!" he called, shouting to make his voice heard over the general clamour.

She saw him and her face lightened. Chivvying the children ahead of her, she made her way through the crowd to him.

"Never, never, have I ever seen such a sight," she said with a gasp and a sigh as she sank down onto the grass at his feet. "So many! So many, Stephen! Did you expect this? Truly?"

"Of course," Stephen exulted, forgetting almost instantly how astounded he himself had been at the sight. "And there will be more, Angeline. More than you can imagine."

For a moment Angeline did not answer. She shook her head. "More? How will you manage such numbers? How will you feed them . . . ?"

But Stephen would hear no doubts.

"God will provide," he said confidently. "He has promised me."

✦ ✦ ✦

They stayed two days in Paris. Stephen preached each morning after the priests had said Mass. As he had hoped, the townspeople lost their suspicions and flocked to hear him. The sun shone down unceasingly and all the omens seemed fair. On the third day they left the city amid tumultuous cheers, their numbers even greater than before. As they made their way out of the city, the bells of the new Cathedral of Notre Dame began to peal, and soon all the other churches and chapels joined in. It was a glorious sound and a heart-lifting one, but as they rode on, Stephen noticed that all who gathered to see them off were not rejoicing. Here and there a mother wept, a father cursed. Stephen turned his eyes away from them. They were misguided. Their children were on their way to glory with him.

That night they slept in the fields surrounding Paris. It was June now and summer was full upon them. The next morning dawned, hazy with heat. They had made their camp near the banks of the River Seine and after the morning Mass, many of the children made their way down to the river to bathe and refresh themselves. Stephen determined to go and fill his waterskins there. A smile teased his lips as he saw Marc and Yves cavorting around as usual. Angeline was watching from the riverbank, Dominic by her side.

Suddenly, Dominic leaped up and raced over to where Marc and Yves were jumping from stone to stone. He tried to imitate them, but the stones were wet. Angeline called to him to come back, but he slipped and fell in the water. Before Angeline could reach him, the current whisked him away. Angeline screamed and ran along the bank beside him, reaching futilely for him.

Stephen was just far enough downstream that the boy was heading straight for him. He dropped his waterskin and plunged into the water, then he lost his footing and fell as well. For one horrible moment he felt himself sucked beneath the surface. The current threw him against one stone and then another. He hit his head. The shock dazed him. The river took hold of him and tumbled him over and over. He could not breathe!

His head broke the surface of the water and he gasped for air, then he sank again. He felt a body bump against him—Dominic! He grabbed hold of the child just as they were swept over a shelf of rock. He managed to surface again long enough to see still water in a pool near the bank. He kicked out with his feet, still hanging on to Dominic. One foot found a purchase on the river bottom and he managed to propel himself and the boy out of the current. Hanging on to Dominic with one hand, he reached for an overhanging branch with the other and managed to take hold of it. A crowd had gathered on the bank. Hands reached out for him, grabbed him, and pulled them out.

Angeline was there to take the child, her face white. Stephen sank down, panting and gasping for air. Dominic threw up a great mouthful of water, then let out a wail.

✦ ✦ ✦

That night, after the children had settled to sleep, Angeline crept to sit beside Stephen.

"That was brave, what you did today," she said.

"It was no more than what I would have done for one of my lambs," Stephen replied.

"But it took courage," Angeline insisted. "Dominic owes his life to you." She fell silent, then spoke again. "I was angry with you when we left St. Denys," she said hesitantly.

"I thought you were," Stephen answered. "You would not ride in the cart with me. Why not?"

"It angered me to see you riding in such comfort when my little ones had to walk," she replied.

"But what can I do?" Stephen asked. "I cannot take them all up with me."

"Perhaps not," Angeline answered.

"Should I not ride then, either?" Stephen asked.

"Of course you should," Angeline said. But she did not sound convinced. "I did not think you would become so—prideful," she added, her voice so low that Stephen was not certain he had heard correctly.

"You think me prideful?" he protested.

"No," she said quickly. "I should not have said that. You are our leader. Of course you should ride." She fell silent. Then she spoke again, slowly, choosing her words carefully as if fearful of offending.

"Can you tell me now, Stephen, what your life was like before you were chosen for this mission?" she asked.

At first Stephen could not find the words to answer her. Finally, staring into the fire, he began to tell her about the fields where he took his sheep, the fields where he had roamed amongst the wreckage and detritus of battle.

"I dreamed then," he said. "I dreamed of the great battles that men had fought for the sake of God. But never did I think that *I* would be chosen to carry out God's will."

"And the man who appeared to you?" Angeline asked. "Who gave you your letter—can you tell me of him?"

"It was not a *man*," Stephen said. He turned to face her. "It was the Christ himself."

"How did you know?" Angeline asked, her voice the barest of whispers.

"I knew," Stephen answered. "I looked into His face and I knew."

"But today," Angeline went on. "Today you might have drowned. What would have happened then? Who would then carry on the mission He gave you?"

"I am doing God's work," Stephen answered. He looked away from her and raised his chin defiantly. "He would not let me die."

But for one instant that day Stephen had thought that he might.

And did Angeline really think he was becoming prideful?

CHAPTER TWELVE

The journey to Vendôme increased Stephen's worries. The weather grew even hotter. No rain fell. The sun beat down upon them unmercifully, and once they left the River Seine behind, there was little water to be found along the way. The small streams that they crossed were, for the most part, dried up. Stephen could see that the fields through which they passed were parched, even this early in the season. Villagers were generous and gave what food they could to the children passing through, but there was not enough. By the time they reached Vendôme almost a week later, many of the children were weak with hunger and exhaustion. Even so, many more had joined along the way, and when they finally drew up to the fields surrounding the city, it was to see thousands of people, young and old, encamped there waiting for them.

"It is an army," Renard whispered in awe.

Stephen leaped to his feet in the cart and steadied himself by grasping onto Renard's shoulder. He swivelled his head from side to side, almost unable to believe what he was seeing. Renard guided the donkey into the midst of the crowd. They were immediately surrounded by a cheering, shouting mass. For a moment, all worry forgotten at the incredible sight, Stephen could do nothing but drink in the glory of it. He had done it! It *was* an army, and *he* had created it. He would prove wrong all those who had doubted him—who had not supported him. He would prove the king of France wrong! Those who followed him would be glorified and praised by Christendom forever.

He felt a surge of triumph and grasped Renard's shoulder even more tightly. Then he took a deep breath and, as Renard brought the cart to a halt, he raised both arms high. Immediately, as if noise had been turned off by an invisible hand, the whole multitude fell silent.

What power I have over them! Stephen exulted. He began to speak.

"My flock!" His voice rang out over the fields. "My faithful followers! Jerusalem *shall* be ours! With faith such as yours we will succeed where our fathers failed. We will march to the edge of the great sea, and there you will see God's promise fulfilled. The waters will part for us and we will walk through them to Jerusalem. Who will dare to oppose us when they see this miracle? Who will not either run from us in terror or fall on their knees to worship the one true God? This I promise you. God wills it!" he cried.

And from thousands of throats the cry echoed back. It echoed in the air, in Stephen's body and in his soul until he was filled with it.

"God wills it! God wills it!"

But then the crowd surged forward. Before Renard could ward them off, two boys clambered onto the cart and tugged at Stephen's tunic.

"Bless me," one of them cried. "You have spoken with our Lord! Give me your blessing!"

"A token," the other clamoured. "I would have a token!"

To Stephen's horror, the boy grasped his hair and pulled a strand out. Stephen raised his hand to his head, shocked at the sudden pain.

"Away!" Renard shouted. "Away with you!"

But even as he cried out, more boys surrounded them. Older people, too, grasped at the cart and rocked it in their frenzy to get near Stephen. Then a woman yanked at the donkey's tail to get a hair from it. At that, the donkey, panicked by the noise and the press of people around it, gave a mighty kick. The woman dodged aside, but another man was not so fortunate. The kick landed squarely on his knee. He fell with a scream of pain. For an instant the crowd drew back. Renard seized the opportunity to whip the donkey into motion. For the first and perhaps the last time in its stubborn life, the donkey surged forward and galloped through the crowd, scattering people left and right. Stephen was thrown back down onto the seat and he held on, stunned, cringing away from grasping hands.

It wasn't until they had found a copse of trees at the farthest edge of the field, that Renard drew the beast to a halt. Trembling, Stephen allowed Renard to help him down. To his relief, no one followed them.

When he knelt to make his confession to Father Martin that night, his stomach still churned. Never had he been so frightened.

"Angeline said I was becoming prideful," he whispered. "She was right. And I have been punished for it."

"Peace, my son," Father Martin answered. "It was not your fault." The words were meant to comfort, but Stephen saw a cloud in the priest's eyes that had not been there before.

✦ ✦ ✦

The abbot of the great Abbey of the Trinity sent for Stephen and Father Martin the following morning. Still shaken by the events of the day before, Stephen followed Father Martin to the abbey steps. There a monk awaited them. Without speaking, the monk gestured for them to follow him. They trailed him through the vast, gloomy aisles of the Abbey, then he pulled aside a curtain covering a doorway and motioned to them to go through into a room carpeted richly and hung with tapestries. Candles burned in sconces on every wall.

The abbot stood, robed and imperious, waiting for him. For a moment Stephen quailed. What if this abbot were no more encouraging than the abbot of St. Denys?

He felt Father Martin's hand squeeze his arm. The priest bowed his head and Stephen made haste to follow suit, his heart thumping in his chest.

Nevertheless, when the abbot spoke, his voice was kindly, his manner friendly.

"Come, Stephen," he said. "Tell me your story."

Still Stephen hesitated. His tongue seemed swollen to twice its size. He stammered. He felt Father Martin give his arm another squeeze and slowly his wits returned to him. He spoke then, and repeated yet again the story of all that had befallen him. As he spoke, the familiar words came more and more easily to him, until finally they poured forth without effort. When he had finished, exhausted, he sank to his knees at the abbot's feet. The abbot laid a hand on his head.

"Go with my blessing, Stephen," he said. "You are doing God's work. Surely He will grant you and your followers a triumph such as Christendom has never seen."

It was with a lighter heart and a firmer step that Stephen made his way back to where Renard had tethered the donkey and Angeline was busy setting the fire. He gave the donkey a grateful scratch behind the ears as he watched the monks giving out chunks of cheese, water, and a knob of bread to every child who asked for it. The lines of waiting children soon stretched across the fields. There seemed to be enough for all, no matter how great the numbers, and the minstrels strolled through the crowd playing and collecting coins. The whole gathering had the atmosphere of a fair. Father Martin and the other priests had issued stern warnings at Mass that morning about endangering Stephen. There was no sign of the previous day's hysteria.

Now, surely, the worst is over, Stephen thought, then jumped as the donkey bit him.

✦ ✦ ✦

They stayed at Vendôme for several weeks. Stephen preached every day, and every day more and more followers joined him. To his surprise, even well-born boys from noble families arrived to join his army, many with their own horses and weapons. Stephen frowned when he saw their shields and swords—his was to be an army that would conquer by faith alone, but these newcomers were proud and haughty and would not think of riding weaponless. Stephen was forced to give in to them if he wanted them to join him—and he did. With knights such as these by his side, people would see how important his crusade was.

Two of them, brothers named Robert and Geoffrey, rode armoured and splendidly attired. Their horses were magnificent, the bridles rang with silver. They were the sons of a great and noble family, they told Stephen, and they had grown up with the shield and sword, the lance and helm of their father, hanging in their great hall. On many a night they had sat and listened to the tales their father told of his crusade to the Holy Land.

"We could not wait to follow in his footsteps and set off on crusade ourselves," Robert said.

"And he gave you his blessing?" Stephen asked.

"He did," Geoffrey answered. "He believed that war in the name of God is man's highest calling. He rode with King Philip on our king's crusade and his only regret was that it had ended in a truce with the Muslim leader Salah-ud-Din."

"A cowardly truce, he called it," Robert put in scornfully. "Agreed to by that dog of an English king, Richard. Our father bade us go forth and avenge the honour of France, and so we have joined you."

"But they seem to be doing it as if it were a favour they grant you," Angeline remarked later as she fed twigs into the evening campfire. "There's little of loyalty there, I think."

"You misjudge them, Angeline, surely," Stephen replied. But in his heart he was not entirely happy with these new followers.

✦ ✦ ✦

When Stephen finally rode out of Vendôme, it was at the head of an exultant army. Red crosses adorned the shoulders or breast of nearly every person who followed him. Many carried the oriflamme, and the flags waved in the light summer breeze. Still more carried crosses, large and small. The prayers and the chanting of the monks and priests put spirit into the soul of every child and adult. In spite of his protests, the two young knights appointed themselves his escort and rode one on either side of him. He had to admit that they did make an impressive sight, but as the noise of their horses' trappings jangled in his ears, it seemed that they cut him off even more from his followers. Renard gloried in it, but when Angeline saw them she turned away with a sniff of disgust.

That night Robert and Geoffrey set up a luxurious tent near where Stephen and Angeline had made camp. They had hired a girl to cook their evening meal for them. Angeline watched their elaborate setting up procedures with tight lips.

"You still do not approve of those two, do you?" Stephen asked, as children held out their bowls to be filled by Angeline.

"They are arrogant," Angeline answered shortly. "They think themselves much too good for the rest of us."

"But they wish to help liberate Jerusalem," Stephen protested. "How could I not make them welcome?"

"They wish to fight," Angeline said stubbornly. "I have heard them talk. They polish their weapons lovingly. I believed we were to conquer the heathens by our faith alone."

Her words stung. They jabbed at Stephen's own misgivings. Perhaps because of that, his reply was curt.

"It is not for you to judge the motives of those who join us," he said. Truth to tell, he was more in awe of the highborn boys than he would like to admit.

Angeline started to reply, but was stopped short by a shout and a cry.

Yves and Marc, of course. In trouble again. The young knights had tethered their horses in a copse of trees beside their tent. One of the animals was rearing up and pawing at the air, snorting and neighing. The shout had come from Robert and the scream from Yves.

"Get away from that horse!" Robert yelled.

Yves was on the ground, shrieking as the horse's hooves plunged into the ground a handsbreadth from his head.

"We just wanted to pat him," wailed Marc, trying in vain to reach his brother.

"You do not pat warhorses!" Geoffrey had emerged from the tent as well and was trying to catch the flying bridle.

Angeline was on her feet in an instant. She ran to Yves and snatched him away just as the horse reared again.

"He is naught but a boy!" she cried. "Control that beast of yours!"

"He'll be a dead boy if I catch him near my horse again," Geoffrey retorted. "If Warrior doesn't kill him, I will."

"You'll not touch him," Angeline shouted, holding Yves close.

"I *will*," Geoffrey retorted.

At that moment the young girl who was making their supper intervened.

"Young masters, will you not sup? Your food is ready." Her soft voice cut through the anger.

The two knights turned their backs on Angeline and stomped over to their fire. The horses moved restlessly and their eyes flared, but they seemed to be quietening.

Stephen followed Angeline. He caught her elbow.

"I'll carry the boy," he said. "Come away, now. Don't make trouble."

"It is not I who am making trouble," Angeline snapped. "And did you see? They had a chicken in their pot. A chicken! I suppose they have coins enough to buy what they want, but not manners enough to share."

Later that evening, just as they were settling down for the night, a figure emerged from the darkness. Stephen looked up, at once wary, then recognized the girl who served Robert and Geoffrey.

"My name is Alys," she said. "I came to see if the lad was all right."

"I believe so," Stephen answered. In truth, he had very little sympathy for Yves.

"He got but a bump on his head," Angeline said as she banked the fire. "He is used to bumps on his head," she added wryly. "He and his brother seem to live for trouble."

"That they most certainly do," Stephen said. He walked a short distance away and settled himself down under a tree. When he finally closed his eyes and slept, Alys and Angeline were still by the remains of the fire, talking.

✦ ✦ ✦

The next morning Alys was back at the knights' camp, setting out bread and cheese for the breaking of their fast.

Stephen watched her for a moment, then turned to Angeline.

"You and that girl talked long last night," he said.

"We did," Angeline replied. "She has had a hard life. Much harder than I. I had a loving mother—until she died. Alys has known nothing but beatings since she was a child. She was abandoned as a babe at an inn. The innkeeper and his wife used her most cruelly. When she heard you speak, you seemed to be a salvation for her."

"And now she serves the young knights as she served her old masters?" Stephen asked, his voice dubious.

"They give her food and they do not beat her," Angeline answered. "She is content with that."

"In Jerusalem . . ." Stephen began, "in Jerusalem she may find a happier life."

"That is what she prays for," Angeline said. She was silent for a moment, then she added quietly. "I think I may have found a friend. I have never had a friend." She turned and began to round up her charges.

Stephen looked after her. He was vaguely irritated, but could not immediately think why. It would be good for Angeline to have a friend, he told himself. Surely he was not jealous? Of a maid?

It was time for Mass. Father Martin would be waiting. This morning Stephen would preach after the Mass. He pushed all other thoughts out of his mind.

CHAPTER THIRTEEN

Although it took only two days to reach the next large village—Blois—it was almost the end of July. The weather continued clear and unbearably hot, with not a drop of rain. The sun shone down upon them without ceasing. They had not found any water along the way and, although the monks of Vendôme had been as generous as they could, there was such a vast number of followers that food was running out yet again. Heat shimmered over the dusty road; children stumbled as they walked. They had passed a swamp, and despite Stephen's warnings, many children could not resist drinking from it and became ill, some of them so severely that they had to be left by the wayside.

"We will get water and sustenance here," Stephen said with relief as Renard drew the cart up by a river that ran through the fields around Blois, but many were so sick and exhausted, they could not drink. They curled up where they stopped and lay there, unmoving.

"We must help them," Angeline said. She encouraged those of her charges who were not too weak to help her fill waterskins and bring them back to the others. When all of her own children had been taken care of, she began to tend to others. Stephen joined her. They worked side by side for the rest of the afternoon.

When the village bells tolled vespers, Stephen paused and looked around. "This is strange," he said. "No one from the village has appeared to help us." He turned to Father Martin. "Come with me, Father, and we will go see why no one has come. We must have food."

But when they walked into the village, they found doors closed against them. The few people they met on the streets turned away.

"We have no food for you," one villager called from within a boarded-up shop. "We have had no rain at all this spring, our crops are withering. There is no food to spare."

"Especially not for an army such as yours," another called. "Move on! There are too many of you! Move on!"

More voices joined them.

"Move on!" they shouted. "Away with you!"

"But we are on God's crusade," Stephen called back. "We are doing the work of the Lord!"

"Then ask the Lord to feed you," a voice behind him cried out. "We have nothing to spare."

Stephen whirled around, but whoever had shouted had disappeared.

Father Martin made the sign of the cross.

"We have many children with us," he called. "Some are ill. They need food. For God's sake, you must help us!"

At that a priest appeared at the end of the street.

"Go back to your camp," he said. "We will see what we can do. But it will not be much. We truly do not have food to spare here. We barely have enough for our own people."

"Thank you," Father Martin said. "God bless you."

But there was not enough to feed even half the number of children who lay sprawled on the stubble of the fields.

"Not even my masters have food," Alys told Stephen. "But they are too proud to line up for this pittance."

"Nor should they," Angeline replied shortly.

That evening Angeline came to Stephen, her face tight.

"Dominic is ill," she said. "He drank of the swamp water and burns now with fever. I have found herbs and tried every remedy my mother ever taught me, but I can do naught."

Stephen followed her to where Dominic lay huddled by a bush. He dropped to his knees and gathered the small body to him. The child was so thin and tiny that he felt almost weightless. Angeline brought a cup of thin broth. Stephen tried to coax Dominic to take a sip, but he could not swallow it. Throughout all the long hours of that night, Stephen held him. Angeline bathed him with water, Stephen dripped water onto his lips, but nothing eased the blazing fever. Toward morning they realized that they would lose him.

"Our littlest one!" Angeline whispered. "The one dearest to my heart! How can I bear it, Stephen?"

"He was one of the first to follow me," Stephen said. He brushed a strand of hair out of Dominic's unseeing eyes. His voice choked. The child had believed in him. Had trusted that Stephen would lead him to a better life.

Stephen looked around at the children sprawled in the fields around him. *How many more will I fail? How many more will I lose?* The questions, black and heavy, swelled inside his head until he thought his skull would burst with the pain.

Dominic died just as the sun rose. Father Martin gave him the last rites, then helped Stephen dig a grave under a tree. Angeline wrapped the small body in her own cloak and laid him carefully in the grave. She stood with head bowed while Stephen and Father Martin filled it in. Father Martin said a short prayer. The other children crowded around—for once even Yves and Marc were silenced.

"He is with God," Father Martin said. But his face was bleak and there was no comfort in his words.

Angeline walked abruptly away. Stephen went after her. Wordlessly, she held out her hand to him and he took it in his. In his burned hand. Scarred and leathery now. He felt her fingers press his, trace the path of the scars, then she gave a terrible sob and turned to bury her face in his shoulder.

✦ ✦ ✦

The villagers were adamant. Stephen and his followers were given no more food. Stephen preached, but few listened. Most lay curled on the grass, listless from the heat and hunger. Flies tormented them incessantly; they did not even have will enough to brush the insects off their faces. With no food to cook, few had bothered to make fires. The men and women in the group, for the most part, still seemed sullen and surly. They kept themselves apart.

"We cannot stay here, Stephen," Father Martin said after Mass the following day. "We must go on, and we must make a choice. I have been told that we can follow this river, which is called the Loire, to the town of Sancerre," Father Martin went on, "or we can leave the river and follow the old road to the town."

"Which is the shortest way?" Stephen asked.

"The old road," Father Martin answered. "But we would be leaving our source of water."

"Let us take the short way," Stephen answered. His desperation made him answer quickly, without thinking. "We will take as much water as we can with us, but we need food. Perhaps the townsfolk of Sancerre will be more generous."

Father Martin looked as if he would argue, then he rolled up his map. "Very well," he said. "Truly one way is as good as the other."

Or as bad, Stephen could not help thinking.

They had not marched more than half a day when they came upon a small stream. It was almost dry, but a trickle of water ran down it. At the head of the procession, Stephen ordered Renard to draw the cart to a halt.

"We will wait here until everyone has refilled their water-skins," he said.

But as soon as the children saw the water, they made a mad dash for it.

"Wait! One at a time!" Stephen cried, but to no avail. Within minutes the bed of the stream had been churned into mud, and what little water there was, rendered undrinkable.

That evening they arrived at another small village. The gates of this village were barred as well. They made camp in the fields, but moved on the next morning when not one person had emerged to offer them food or water, not even a priest.

The day after that they found another stream bed. This one was completely dry. By this time many of the water-skins and containers that they had filled in Blois were empty. Some of the older men dug to see if they could find water, but there was none. The sun beat down upon them, hour after hour, out of a hard blue sky. They made camp there anyway, too exhausted to go on.

"Have the children look for wild berries and roots," Angeline said.

The children brought back what they could find, but it was pitifully little. Stephen feared that they were raiding the fields through which they passed as well, but he chose not to see it. The more resourceful boys snared rabbits. Finally, even Renard was forced by the hunger in his belly to help. He brought back two rangy hares. Angeline took them from him immediately and skewered them on sticks over the fire. She placed a pot under them to catch the fat and juices that dripped out as the animals cooked.

"The children first," she said. "They need these more than we do."

Renard's share was so small that he threw it back at her.

"When next I hunt, you will not see the results of it," he snarled and stomped back into the woods.

"He is more trouble than he is worth," Angeline said. She beckoned to a small girl and spooned the extra bite of meat into the child's mouth. "I could wish he had never joined us."

Stephen said nothing, but in his heart he could not help but agree. But what could he do? Renard had answered his call—he could not force him to leave.

In his prayers that night he could find no solace, and deep within him, a furtive, terrifying fear was taking root. Had he somehow sinned? Had God deserted them?

The following day, when they found yet another village barred against them, Stephen could bear it no longer.

"Drive the cart hard against the walls," he ordered Renard. Then he leaped down and beat upon the gate.

"We are God's army!" he yelled. "You *must* help us!" But the only answer was a solitary voice from behind the wall.

"We have no food for you. Go away!"

"There is a good-sized river just a half-day's journey from here," Father Martin said, smoothing his map with hands that shook. "Surely there will be water there."

They could see dusty trees lining the river as they drew near. Renard urged the donkey into a limping trot, but when they reached the riverbank it was to see a dry bed covered with stones.

"We must camp here anyway," Stephen said. "The children have not the strength to go on." He eased himself down from the cart, his own knees weak from hunger. Renard saw to unhitching the donkey, who began scrabbling for grass and any moisture it could find.

Would that we could eat grass, Stephen thought.

"Your two noble knights have water enough," Angeline said bitterly. "I saw them giving some to their horses."

Stephen made the rounds the next morning, sharing the water that he had husbanded so carefully, and ensuring to the best of his ability that those who still had some shared it as well, but he knew that many of the men and women who had joined them hid what they had.

Stephen's fears grew with regards to some of the older people. Many of the men were rough and cruel-looking and several of the women were coarse and vulgar. They looked to be cast up from the very dregs of the cities and towns through which they passed.

"Their motives for joining us cannot be good," Father Martin grumbled. "They will not swear the oath, most do not even bother to wear the cross."

"They worry me, too, Father," Stephen said.

That night Stephen could not sleep. He was losing control. Things were happening that he could do nothing about. How long would this go on? He prayed for relief for his followers. Surely God would hear him.

By the fifth day after they had left Blois, they had still not found water. When they stopped for a rest at midday, Stephen sank down on the dried-out grass. He shook his waterskin. A small gurgle. Beside him, Father Martin sank down as well. Stephen held out the waterskin to the priest, but Father Martin shook his head.

"Give it to the children," he whispered.

Stephen looked at him. Father Martin's face was gaunt, his eyes huge and staring. His hair was matted and hanging over his eyes.

He looks half-crazed, Stephen thought. *And so must I.*

More children died that day. There was no thought of burying them; they could only be left by the roadside. The ground was too hard and dry; no one had the strength in any case. If they were fortunate, a priest or a monk would see them fall and give them a final blessing, but all were left where they dropped as the others trudged on.

Around the middle of the day, when they stopped to rest, Robert and Geoffrey accosted Stephen.

"We have run out of water for our horses," Robert said.

"They are fine beasts," Geoffrey put in. "The finest in our father's stables. You cannot allow them to be so mistreated."

"I cannot give them water when children are dying for the lack of it," Stephen said. "What little I have remaining must be for them. My donkey suffers also."

"Donkey!" Robert exclaimed. "What is a donkey compared to our horses?"

At that, Stephen could take no more.

"Did not our Lord ride into Jerusalem on a donkey?" he cried. "Do you dare call yourselves Christians?"

He was rewarded by seeing them look ashamed and they said no more, but the next morning his last goatskin of water was missing.

+ + +

The next day yet another village barred their gates to them.

"I must do something!" Stephen said. He rubbed the back of his hand across his forehead. Then he turned to Robert and Geoffrey.

"Leave me," he ordered. "Go and make your camp." As they rode off, he turned to Renard. "Give me the reins," he said.

Renard handed the reins over, puzzled.

Stephen urged the donkey forward. The poor beast could hardly move. Stephen flapped the reins at it again, but it stopped in its tracks. Nothing Stephen could do would persuade it to go forward again.

"Lead it," Stephen ordered Renard. "To the village gate."

"But they have already turned us away," Renard protested.

"Do as I say," Stephen repeated. He had not the energy to argue.

Renard took the donkey's reins without further argument and pulled it toward the village.

At the gate, a keeper barred their way.

"I have told you, there is no food for you," the gatekeeper snarled. "Get your horde away from here!"

"I am not begging for food now," Stephen said. "I am bartering. I will trade the donkey and the cart for any food and water that you can give me"

Renard stared at Stephen in dismay, but a greedy light lit up the gatekeeper's eyes.

"Anything?" he asked.

"Anything," Stephen answered. He passed over the empty waterskins.

The keeper disappeared.

"Surely you cannot mean this?" Renard demanded. "You would give away our cart? Our donkey?"

"We need food, Renard," Stephen answered shortly.

"But," Renard protested, "what will we do without them?"

"We will walk," Stephen answered.

A short time later the man reappeared, bearing a sack. Another man accompanied him, carrying the waterskins. The skins were loose and half empty.

"Bread is all we can spare," the man said. "And precious little water. Our well is running dry."

A pitiful exchange for a donkey and cart, but Stephen was desperate.

"You said you would take anything," the gatekeeper began, expecting an argument.

"I did," Stephen answered. He got down from the cart and signalled to Renard to do likewise. He walked over to the man and held his arms out for the sack. "I meant it."

CHAPTER FOURTEEN

When Stephen and Renard returned to the field where Father Martin waited, the rest of Stephen's followers were straggling in. Father Martin's face was purple with the heat, but he and some of the other priests and monks were going from group to group, sharing out the last sips of water. Stephen gave Father Martin the sack of bread and some of the waterskins.

"Where are the cart and donkey?" Father Martin asked.

"I traded them," Stephen answered, and tried to ignore the priest's look of surprise. Did Father Martin think the cart and beast were so important to him? Then, with a flush of shame, Stephen realized that the priest had every right to think so.

He looked around for Angeline, but she was nowhere to be seen. She had been disdainful of the luxury he had been so pleased to indulge in—*she* would approve of his trading it for food. The thought almost gave him pleasure enough to compensate for the loss, but he hoped the donkey's new master was kind. He had grown fond of the beast in spite of its ill nature.

It was not until much later that Angeline walked into the camp, however. She trudged along with her head down, seemingly oblivious to the small group of children that trailed her. This was not like her at all. Stephen stared at her. Her clothes were little more than rags by now, and she was barefoot. She was dirtier than she had ever been and she looked gaunt and ill. He called to her, but she seemed not to hear. Troubled, Stephen made his way through the horde of people that were settling down and making their campsites for the night. The field was already overrun and trodden by the hundreds of feet, and strewn with garbage. Scrawny, half-starved dogs ran here and there in between the campsites, scavenging for whatever pitiful scraps they could find. The encampment was eerily silent. No singing now, not even the usual cacophony of shouts, cries, and curses. No one had the energy for it. Stephen stopped for a moment to share his waterskin with a small child who lay motionless beside an older girl. When he offered the skin to the girl she grabbed it, and before he could stop her, drained it dry. Stephen started to reprimand her, then stopped. He could not bring himself to chastise her.

He reached Angeline's side and held out his hand, but she ignored it.

"What is the matter?" he asked.

Angeline looked back at him with hollow eyes that seemed far too big for her face. The incandescent light that had so mesmerized Stephen on that first day, had gone out. Her eyes looked dead. And sad beyond belief.

"Yves and Marc died today," she said. "They just lay down and died in each other's arms. I could not bury them. The ground is too hard. I scratched at it with my spoon, but I could not make a hole big enough. I had to leave them there. All alone."

She dropped to the ground. Stephen sank down beside her. He started to put an arm around her shoulders, to comfort her, then dropped it, unsure as to whether she would want him to do so.

"What can we do, Stephen?" Angeline asked.

Stephen hesitated for a long moment. How to answer her? How could he give her strength when he truly had none left himself?

"I know it is hard," he said finally. "But we must go on." He was stopped by the look on her face. "What else *can* we do?" he pleaded, almost desperately.

"That is all you can say?" Angeline demanded. She lifted her head and her eyes blazed for a moment. "Children are dying every day! Dominic, Yves, Marc . . . so many others. . . . You must do *something*, Stephen. You *have* to do something!"

Stephen felt his heart twist with pain.

"I cannot provide food when there is none to be had!" he burst out. "I cannot make dry rivers fill with water!"

"You said this was God's crusade," Angeline insisted, her voice shrill. "You said the Lord would provide. You promised!"

"And you said you could endure whatever suffering we might face," Stephen shot back.

"And so I can," Angeline cried. "It is for the little ones that I grieve."

"Pray for them then," Stephen said. "That is all we can do. We must pray for them."

"God can make a headless man walk," Angeline spat out the words, "but he cannot feed His innocent children?"

"How dare you!" Stephen cried, torn beyond endurance. "How dare you question our Lord's wisdom?"

Brave words, but he had to leap quickly to his feet and stride away before she could see the tears that brimmed in his eyes.

✦ ✦ ✦

Stephen walked with the others when they left the next morning. Robert and Geoffrey gave him a contemptuous look and hastened to ride with the other young knights at the head of the procession, leaving Alys to walk with Angeline.

"Am I being punished for my pride?" Stephen asked Father Martin. Before the priest could answer Angeline broke in.

"It is not you who is being punished," she said. "It is the dead children we leave behind us who are being punished."

Stephen bit his lip and said no more. When he came to a small boy sitting by the side of the road, he scooped him up and carried him.

✦ ✦ ✦

Matters grew even worse over the next few days. They found water at a river that Father Martin's map identified as the Sauldre, but the only food to be had was what could be found in the woods or what could be stolen from some luckless farmer's field. Stephen did not even bother to turn his head away so as not to see the thievery. Surely God would forgive them. No villagers came out to offer food. Not even the haughty young knights could find any who would exchange food for their coins. The fields through which they passed were dry and sere. What crops had managed to grow were stunted and sparse. To Stephen's dismay, when he looked back he could see that though more children died every day, his followers were still so numerous that besides taking what they could, often they trampled the few remaining crops. He looked at the ruination and hardened his heart against the guilt that threatened to

overcome him. The needs of his crusade must take precedence. It was God's will.

Finally, they reached the Loire again. Stephen set down
the child he had been carrying and the boy ran to join the
hordes of children who plunged into the water with shouts
and cries of joy. As they made their camp by the riverbank,
the skies clouded over and it began to rain. Stephen lifted
his face to the merciful wetness and gave thanks. There was
still no food, but there was water. That evening, for the first
time in days, Stephen preached.

They marched on the next morning and reached the
town of Sancerre by evening. Here, at last, Stephen found
his prayers answered. The drought had not been as bad in
these parts, and the townsfolk came out to them, bringing
whatever they could give.

"We have heard of your crusade," one elder said to Stephen. "We have been expecting you and we will help you as
best we can."

And help they did. Food was given to them unstintingly.
Grain was brought for the horses. Robert and Geoffrey
finally stopped grumbling and set Alys to work cooking
their evening meal. Village fishermen caught fish in the river
and brought them to Stephen by the basketful. Angeline
cooked and boiled and smiled for the first time in weeks, as
she ladled out bowlfuls of rich, hearty soup.

Stephen preached after Mass that evening. Stomach full,
looking out over the crowd of smiling faces, he preached
with renewed faith and vigour.

"God has not deserted us," he cried. "Nor will He! We have
passed the test. We have survived. We *will* reach Jerusalem!"

The roar that greeted his words filled his soul with as
much strength as had the food that filled his belly.

The villagers were generous, but for many of the children
it was too late. Hunger and sickness had taken their toll.

When Stephen's crusade departed, they left behind a score more of small bodies buried under the trees. The villagers lent them shovels with which to dig graves. The priests gave the last rites.

It was small consolation.

✦ ✦ ✦

They followed the River Loire south. Water was no longer a problem, but food remained so. Some villages overwhelmed them with generosity, giving all they had, but others shut their gates and bade them be gone. There was never enough.

"The children are still dying," Angeline said. Stephen tried not to hear.

"I must speak to you," Father Martin said one night. His face was grim.

"What is it now, Father?" Stephen replied. He could not keep the weariness out of his voice.

"These older people in our company . . ." the priest began.

Stephen waited for what the priest would say with a sinking heart.

" . . . some of them are good, devout Christians, and they help the younger ones as best they can," Father Martin said. "But not all. There are some who prey on the smaller ones. They steal food. They steal what clothing the children have. And worse."

"Worse?" Stephen echoed. He did not want to hear what the priest would say next.

"Worse," Father Martin repeated. "They force the children to do their will. They make slaves of them."

Though Stephen wished with all his heart not to believe the priest's words, he could not help but do so. He also had seen men, and women too, who abused the smaller ones around them. He stopped it when he saw it happening, but he knew that there must be much going on that he could not prevent. The brief surge of elation he had felt at Sancerre had ebbed. Again, he felt the worms of doubt eating at his soul.

"Have I been misled, Father?" he asked. "Have I been duped—perhaps even used as a tool of the devil himself as that priest said? Was King Philip right and I wrong? I, the arrogant one?"

Father Martin sat for a long time before replying. Stephen awaited his words with a sinking heart. If Father Martin had given up, then all was certainly lost.

"I do not think so, Stephen," he said at last.

The words were the ones Stephen wished to hear, but the tone of voice in which they were spoken offered little reassurance.

"I do not think so," the priest repeated slowly. And then he echoed Stephen's own words to Angeline. "Who are we to question the ways of the Lord?"

"But what of all those innocents who trusted in me?" Stephen asked. "Who believed my promises, and who died?" He could not keep the anguish out of his voice.

"Those little ones are with God now," Father Martin replied.

"But they suffered," Stephen said. "They suffered, and those who still live suffer as well. How can I justify that?"

"It is not for you to justify anything," Father Martin replied. His voice was stern. "Did not Jesus suffer? The Lord gave you a commandment, you must obey it. This is a wondrous task you have been set, Stephen. Who would ever have believed that a boy such as you would have been chosen by God for such a venture?" As he spoke, his voice grew stronger, more exultant. "I prayed for so long for another crusade, but never did I imagine that *I* would be so blessed by God that I would be allowed to be a part of it. You must have faith, Stephen. You must not waver!"

Stephen subsided into silence. He believed Father Martin. He *had* to believe him. But the sound of a nearby child sobbing in tired desperation ate into his very soul.

✦ ✦ ✦

One day, as they made camp, Stephen realized that Angeline was not with them.

"I think she stopped to rest," Father Martin said. "She will certainly catch up to us later."

But she did not reappear and Stephen grew increasingly worried.

"I am going to walk back a bit," he said to Father Martin.

"I will come with you," the priest said. He, too, looked anxious.

They made their way back against the flow of children. Stephen was shocked all over again to see how dispirited and exhausted they were. No singing now. No noise at all. They had not enough energy left even to talk. But, as Stephen and Father Martin rounded a bend, they saw a knot of men and women and heard raucous laughter. They were watching someone or something on the ground. As Stephen and the priest drew near, they realized with horror what the source of the group's coarse amusement was.

Angeline lay on the ground. A bearded, heavyset man was crouched above her. He had pinned her arms down, and as Stephen and Father Martin watched, shocked, he threw himself upon her.

Stephen ran forward, but Father Martin was too quick for him. The priest snatched up a stick from the ground and charged at the man, his black robe flying. He swung the stick at his back with all the force he could muster.

"Be off with you!" he cried. "Swine! Worse than swine! Be off with you, I say!"

He laid about him with the stick, hitting everyone indiscriminately, until the women screamed and the men ran.

Stephen rushed to Angeline's side. She lay white and still, her eyes closed.

"Bring water," Father Martin commanded a boy who was standing near, open-mouthed.

The boy sprinted off and returned with a wet cloth. Father Martin began to bathe Angeline's face. Stephen reached for her hand. Only when she opened her eyes did he breathe again.

"I thought you to be dead," he said.

✦ ✦ ✦

That night Stephen would not let Angeline make the evening soup. He insisted that she sit while Alys and he fed the little ones, then he brought a bowl of the thin broth to her. He sat by her and watched anxiously as she ate.

"Are you certain you are all right?" he asked. "You are not hurt?"

"I am well," Angeline answered, but the tone of her voice gave the lie to her words. No matter how much Stephen tried to console her, she sat cold and frozen with shock. Finally, he could bear it no longer. He dropped his head into his hands. His shoulders shook.

"It was not supposed to be like this," he whispered. "It was not supposed to be like this."

CHAPTER FIFTEEN

The sun beat down with an ever increasing intensity. Even with water, the children still suffered intolerably from the heat and lack of food. Some sank down on the road, exhausted, and could not be made to get up. Those, too, they had to leave.

Then the land began to rise in gentle hills. Stephen's foreboding increased.

"There are mountains ahead of us," Father Martin said.

"How high?" Stephen asked. Stephen had never seen mountains. He could not really imagine what they were like.

"I do not know how high they are. The map does not say," Father Martin answered. Then he added, "We are going to have to leave the river again."

"But we need the water," Stephen protested.

"Nevertheless, we must leave it and go eastwards to Lyons," the priest said. "It is the only way. But there are certain to be streams in the mountains, and Lyons lies on the bank of another great river, the Rhône. We will be able to follow it all the way to Marseilles. Water will not be a problem."

"But first we must cross the mountains?" Stephen asked.

"First we must cross the mountains," Father Martin answered. "At least at this time of the year there should not be snow, I am told."

✦ ✦ ✦

It was well into the month of August when they made the turn eastward toward the mountains some days later. In spite of Father Martin's assurances, Stephen could not help but look back at the Loire, as they left it, with regret and with trepidation. The road they followed now was narrow and steep. Ahead of them, he could see high crests and peaks of mountains. It was true that there was no snow, nevertheless the air cooled as they climbed. At first it was a relief from the relentless heat, but they were forced to camp that night in an area made dangerous with steep cliffs and ravines. Father Martin had been right, there were mountain streams to supply them with water and that was welcome, but they were so cold and icy that the runoff from them made the path slippery and treacherous.

"Take the word back that children are not to leave the path," Stephen ordered Renard.

Alys had not been able to keep up with Robert and Geoffrey, so she stayed with Angeline and helped keep her group safe, while Father Martin searched out the waterways and filled their waterskins.

Stephen sat huddled by Angeline's group. He did not sleep. He could not watch over all of his followers, but at least he could safeguard Angeline. She had not spoken of the attack upon her, but gradually she had begun to come back to herself. Stephen, however, was at a loss as to what to say to her. He did not know what would comfort her, what would anger her. In his confusion, he had even found himself avoiding her during the day.

Now, he started as he felt a hand upon his shoulder. It was Angeline. For a long while she sat beside him in silence, then finally she spoke, but it was not to talk of the assault.

"Look, Stephen," she said instead. "Look at the stars in the heavens above us."

The moon broke free of a cloud just then, and in its silvery light he could see that she sat with her head thrown back. He followed her gaze upwards. The last few remaining clouds had cleared away and it was as if he were looking down instead of up. Down into a bowl of midnight blackness, pinpointed with tiny, impossibly brilliant stars.

"It is so vast, is it not?" Angeline asked.

"It is," Stephen answered.

"And we are so small," Angeline went on.

"Small, but not insignificant," Stephen replied.

"No, not insignificant," Angeline agreed. "In God's sight we are all important, are we not?"

"We are," Stephen answered.

"That is what the priests say," Angeline said. "I never had much use for priests. Our village priest treated my mother badly, and she did not deserve it. Father Martin is kind, though, isn't he?"

"He is," Stephen said. He spoke cautiously, choosing his words with care, almost as if he feared that one misspoken word would frighten her off.

"I owe him much," Angeline said. "If it were not for him . . ." her voice trailed off.

"I owe him much as well," Stephen said.

"Yes," Angeline agreed. "He has helped you greatly on this crusade."

"He has," Stephen said. "I could not have come this far without him." But that was not what he had meant. Not what he was thinking.

I owe him much because he saved you. I could not go on without you.

That was what he was thinking. The thought was a revelation. He was stunned by it. When had this happened?

✦ ✦ ✦

The next morning the priests said Mass, but hurriedly. All wanted to be moving on and through the mountains as quickly as possible.

It was with relief that they set out, but the relief soon changed to fear. As they climbed, the air grew increasingly cold. Most of the little ones wore nothing but rags. Many had no cloak to keep them warm, and others were barefoot. The second night they spent in the mountains found them huddling together for warmth, trying to find shelter from the biting wind in whatever nook or cranny they could find. During that night many of the older ones foreswore their vows and deserted to return to the warmer lands they had left. Stephen could not fault them; he only hoped that they made it there.

The morning after that, Stephen had the priests say Mass even earlier—before the sun's rays found their way down to them. He was in a frenzy to get away from these terrible mountains, back into the warmth. Lyons lay within a day's march, Father Martin had told him. It was a large and prosperous city—surely there they would find the food and assistance that they needed.

It took prodding and force to get the children moving again. Many, stupefied by the cold, were reluctant to get up. Even Renard balked until Angeline gave him a disdainful kick. But that day they began to descend and the path grew easier. Spirits rose with the temperature. Finally, they rounded the last turn of the twisting road and there before them lay the city of Lyons, nestled between the Rhône and the Saone rivers.

"Is that Jerusalem?" a small voice asked from behind Stephen.

"Not yet," Stephen answered. "But the worst is over, I am certain of it." He tried not to remember that he had thought that before.

+ + +

Lyons was truly a great city, thronged with people. Priests and monks strode about the streets, merchants and traders plied their wares on every corner. Stephen was still not used to such big cities, and after the silence of the mountains, he felt assaulted with the noise and smells. Here they did receive the sustenance they so badly needed, however. Father Martin led them to a great cathedral and there they were met by the archbishop of Lyons himself.

"You are welcome," the archbishop announced. "We have been waiting for you and have made arrangements for your comfort. The churches and the cathedrals of the city are open to your followers to sleep in tonight. My priests will lead them there. You may also take shelter in the old Roman amphitheatre," he added, gesturing to the ruins of a great, circular stone building that looked down upon the city and the cathedral where they stood.

Stephen looked up at the crumbling walls in awe. "It looks very old," he said.

"It is," the archbishop replied. "The Romans ruled here many centuries ago and they constructed wondrous buildings." For a moment an uneasy look crossed his face. "They were pagans," he said, "but they finally converted to the true faith."

"What happened to them?" Stephen asked.

"They came as conquerors, and they in turn were conquered by others who came after them," the archbishop answered.

"It seems that war is the way of the world," Angeline put in from behind Stephen.

"War in God's name is holy," the archbishop said, crossing himself.

To Stephen's relief, Angeline said no more.

The priests came out to where Stephen's followers were gathered in a field outside the town, bringing bread and cheese. Then, as the archbishop had promised, the priests led them, children and adults alike, into the town. Stephen hung back until he had seen all cared for. One of the archbishop's priests waited with Father Martin. Angeline and Renard stayed back as well.

Stephen looked up at the hill above the city where the ancient ruins stood. It was a steep climb—none of the others had chosen to take refuge there. He turned to the group that waited upon him.

"You should go with this priest," he said. "Seek your shelter in the town. I would spend the night up in those ruins."

"I will go with you," Angeline said quickly.

Renard cast her a jealous glance. "No," he said. "*I* shall."

Stephen raised a hand to silence them both. He turned to Father Martin. "Have my followers assemble in the field tomorrow morning for Mass, Father. I will come back then." He could not explain, even to Angeline, how he felt, but he needed to be alone this night. He had much to mull over.

He watched until they disappeared beyond the city gates, then began to climb. By the time he reached the crumbling walls of the old ruins, he was winded, but as he turned to look at the city tucked in between the rivers, he caught his breath with the magnificence of the view.

The air was clear, dusk just falling. Fires flickered here and there within the city. It was the first time he had been alone since he had left Cloyes. Stephen drank in the silence and the solitude as if it were nourishment. Just so had he sat by himself all the days while he tended his sheep. Sat and dreamed impossible dreams. Impossible dreams that had now come true.

At that thought all peace deserted him. No, the dreams he had dreamed had not come true. He had dreamed of glorious battles and victories in the name of God. He had not dreamed of the suffering and death of innocents.

He sat there until the darkness enveloped the city and the fires winked out one by one, then he settled himself in a grassy nook between the stones. Perhaps God would speak to him again this night. Reassure him that the path he followed was the right one.

But it was not to be. His dreams that night were restless and disturbed. Several times he awoke, fancying that he heard screams. When the sun finally sent out its first rays he rose, stiff and sore in body and mind, and made his way back to the field where his followers awaited him.

After Mass, at which the archbishop himself presided, Stephen stood up to preach. He leaped up onto a wall and lifted his arms to the sky, then opened his palms to ask for silence. Only when the last murmurings faded away, did he begin to speak.

"We march now to Marseilles," he cried. "The worst of our travails is past. You, who have suffered so much but who have persevered with such faith and devotion, will receive your reward. You will stand with me and watch the waters of the great sea that lies between Marseilles and the Holy Land part for us. God has promised me this. We will watch the waters part and then we will walk between their shining walls to Jerusalem. Our victory is near. God wills it!"

Once again the cry arose from every throat: "God wills it! God wills it!"

But when the priests began to distribute food and the children raced to receive it, Father Martin drew Stephen aside.

"You do not look well," he said.

"I could not sleep," Stephen answered. "I had dreams— heard strange things . . . ."

"I do not wonder," Father Martin answered. "That amphitheatre was a place of evil. If I had known, I would have stopped you from going there."

"Of evil?" Stephen asked. "But the archbishop said the Romans built wondrous buildings!"

"So they did, but before they converted to the true faith they persecuted Christians. In places such as that they killed Christians in barbarous ways. Forced them to fight each other. Forced them to fight and be torn to pieces by wild beasts. That is a place soaked in the blood of Christian martyrs, Stephen."

✦ ✦ ✦

The townspeople of Lyons were generous, but they made it very clear that Stephen and his followers would not be welcome for more than two days.

"We have been pleased to follow God's commandment to give you succour to the best of our ability, but there are too many of you to take care of for any longer," the archbishop said.

"We thank you for what you have given us," Stephen replied, kneeling before him. "You have been more than generous."

"We have but done as our Lord commands us," the archbishop replied. "You go with my blessing."

The third day they set out again, following Father Martin's map.

"We are on one of the ancient Roman roads now," the priest told Stephen. "I am told it is called the Via Agrippa. It goes south following the Rhône valley. We will have all the water we need as long as we keep close to the river."

Stephen could see even higher mountains to the east that were still snow-capped. He gave thanks to God in a silent prayer that they would not have to cross those.

The river provided them with water, but again and as always, food was a problem. Some villages were generous, others shut their gates to them and ordered them to be on their way. The farther south they went, the softer the weather grew, and the fields around them were more lush. Here the people had been spared the drought. Breezes carrying foreign, tantalizing scents sprang up to cool them; the sun shone more gently. The road rose and fell in small hills as they passed through Avignon, Provence, and Aix. They were treated with kindness and given food in all three towns. The children were weak, however, their steps faltering. Still, it seemed to Stephen as if he could smell the sea. A current began to run through the whole crusade. A feeling of expectancy.

But it seemed that the closer they got to the sea, the more disturbed Angeline became. One night, as they sat by the fire together, she was restless. Almost irritably, she poked at the fire after Stephen had banked it for the night. As the flames flared up again, Stephen looked at her inquiringly.

"There is something bothering you, is there not?" he asked.

For a moment Angeline did not answer, then she sat back and looked at him. The flames cast shadows on her face. He could not see her eyes.

"This sea," she said slowly. "I fear it. Is it truly big?"

"It is, so I have been told," Stephen replied.

"How . . . ? How then, will we be able to walk across it?" Angeline asked.

"Do you doubt that the sea parted for Moses and the children of Israel, and that they walked across it?" Stephen asked.

"No . . ." Angeline answered, but she sounded uncertain. "That is what we have been taught . . ." The words trailed off.

"God has promised me that even as He made the waters part for Moses, He will part them for me," Stephen said. "It will be *glorious*, Angeline. Just wait. It will be glorious."

He had to think that. He could not let himself think anything else.

CHAPTER SIXTEEN

The next afternoon they climbed one more hill and there at last lay the sea—a shimmering expanse of blue-green water that stretched to the horizon. Under a clear blue sky dotted with white clouds, the waters spread out before them in tranquil waves. Strange, fan-leafed trees lined the shore and swayed in the soft breeze. At the foot of the cliffs upon which they stood sprawled a busy, bustling town. Marseilles!

They had done it.

Beside him, Stephen heard a sharp intake of breath and he turned to see Father Martin. The priest's eyes were bright with tears.

"Give thanks to the Lord, Stephen," the priest said.

"I do," Stephen replied. His heart was so full he could say no more.

They knelt to pray. Angeline and Renard knelt with them, but at the sight of the sea, Stephen's followers could not be restrained. Young and old, they began to run down the paths toward it. Robert and Geoffrey and the other young knights galloped past them. Stephen grimaced as he saw one young boy knocked aside by a horse in the rush. He ran to him and picked him up, but the boy was unhurt. In just as much of a rush to get to the sea as all the others, he was off without so much as a word of thanks. No one had told the children that the waters of this sea were salt, however. Father Martin ran after them, calling to them.

"Drink not the water!" he shouted.

Too late. Children spat and shook their heads, unable to believe that such a great expanse of water was not available to them to slake their thirst. Help was at hand, however. The news of their arrival had gone ahead of them, for the bells of all the churches of Marseilles began to peal. First one, then another, then another joined in until the very heavens seemed to echo with their ringing. By the time Stephen reached the rocky beach, the townspeople were flooding out to meet them, carrying all manner of food and drink. Bread, cheese, cold fowl, and fruits Stephen had never seen before. The children swarmed the people, and were greeted with smiles and laughter.

Stephen left Angeline to try to bring order to the melée on the beach and strode toward the city gate, Father Martin close beside him. As they reached the gate a boy ran out to greet them, panting.

"Are you the one they call Stephen?" he panted. "The one sent by God?"

"I am," Stephen replied and with the words he was overcome with a joy such as he had never known. The sun blazing down upon them was brighter than he had ever seen it. The air crystal clear and pure. His every sense tingled with the glory of the moment.

The boy seemed suddenly struck dumb.

"The bishop," he finally managed to get out, while bobbing his head and tripping himself up, trying to bow at the same time. "The bishop will speak with you." He stopped and drew a deep breath. "He wishes me to lead you to him. Follow me. Please," he added.

Father Martin reached out to give Stephen's shoulder a squeeze. The smile on his face was as broad as the smile on Stephen's own.

They followed the boy to the rectory adjoining the basilica. There the bishop waited in the company of another stern-looking man who, the boy whispered, was the count of Provence himself, the ruler of the county of Provence in which Marseilles was situated. Bursting with triumph, Stephen was not in the least daunted by their presence. He made his obeisance, then stood proudly, awaiting their words. Words of praise they would be, he was certain of it. After all, had he not succeeded in leading his crusade all the way across France?

The bishop's first words did, indeed, bear out Stephen's confidence.

"We have heard much of your crusade, Stephen," the bishop said. "The very fact that you have led such an enormous number of people to the shores of our sea is most impressive."

Stephen basked in the words. The bishop went on.

"We will supply you and your followers with all that you need tonight," he continued. "Even though such a great number of people will strain our resources, your followers will be fed. As many as possible will be allowed to sleep in our cathedral, in the abbey, and here in the Basilique St. Victor. Even so, I fear that we will not be able to accommodate so great a number of souls, but I am certain that the townspeople, too, will welcome the children and give them shelter."

Stephen began to thank him, but the bishop continued.

"However . . ." he said.

Stephen stopped short, the words of gratitude dying in his mouth.

"However," the bishop repeated, "we can only offer this assistance for one night. There are simply too many of you to welcome within this city for any longer."

"There will be no need," Stephen replied quickly. "If you have heard of this crusade, you will also have heard of the promise our Lord gave to me. On the morrow, just shortly after the sun has risen, I will stand on the shore of the sea and the waters will part for us. You will watch as we walk through them, untouched." He could not help the pride that crept into his voice. He saw the bishop's face close.

"Do you really believe this will happen?" the bishop asked.

"Of course," Stephen replied indignantly. "Do you not believe the promises of the Lord, whom you serve?"

Father Martin hissed in distress and grabbed at his arm, but Stephen shook him off. The bishop frowned. The count, beside him, made a move almost as if to strike Stephen for his insolence, but Stephen stood his ground. He it was who had followed God's command and led his army here. He was not afraid of these men.

"God knows I hope and pray that you are not misled, my son," the bishop said. He made the sign of the cross in blessing, then waved at Stephen to depart. "I will be there tomorrow," he said, "to witness your miracle." His voice made it very apparent how unlikely he thought that would be.

Stephen seethed at the insult.

Just wait, he vowed silently, teeth clenched. *Just wait until the morn. Then you will see that I speak the truth. The whole city will see!*

✦ ✦ ✦

Stephen returned to the beach. He climbed up onto a
rock and raised his arms high. Slowly, the crowd began to
assemble around him. He waited until they had all gathered. He waited until the throng fell silent. He felt a rush
of love flood through him as he looked down upon them,
young and old alike. He had fulfilled his promise to them!
Finally, he drew breath and let his words come forth with a
rush of power.

"You will all be given food and a place to sleep tonight,"
he cried. "Rest and refresh yourselves. Tomorrow at dawn,
come back. God's promise will be fulfilled. The waters will
part for us and we will walk through them to Jerusalem!
The end of our journey is at hand, and you will be well
rewarded. *God wills it!*"

This time his cry was triumphant. The townsfolk's cries
joined his, louder and louder until the cliffs rang with the
sound. The very birds of the air that wheeled and swooped
around them seemed to Stephen to be exulting with him.
He watched as the crowd began to disperse and make their
way into the city. Father Martin and Renard stood beside
him. Robert and Geoffrey had long since left to find proper
quarters in the town. He saw a stout, motherly woman
approach Angeline and Alys. The woman was obviously
offering shelter to the two girls.

For a moment Stephen felt a pang. He did not want
Angeline to leave. He had thought that she would stay with
him this last night. Then, with relief, he saw that she was
not going with Alys and the woman. She gave Alys a hug
and turned back toward him. He greeted her with an outstretched hand.

He could not eat that night, however, although Renard
had procured ample food. There was even, much to Father
Martin's delight, a skin of wine. Angeline boiled a chicken
in a pot over the fire. She had seen all of her charges off

with various kindly women, and for once, she was able to rest and eat. Nothing she said could tempt Stephen, however. It was enough for him that she was here with him, but his mind, his spirit were full of the glory of the miracle that he would cause to happen in the morning. He had no need of food.

✦ ✦ ✦

After the priests had said Mass, as the sun rose the next morning, Stephen stood on the pebbly sand of the shore. Behind and all around crowded the thousands upon thousands of his followers. The townspeople of Marseilles were there as well, shops and stalls were closed for the event. He saw the bishop and the count under one of the palm trees, watching intently. He swallowed and tried to quell the nausea that tightened his belly. Now, finally, it was time. He took a step forward until he stood ankle deep in the sea. He wanted to feel it as it withdrew. The hum of voices ceased. The multitude surrounding him fell silent. The sound of the sea filled his ears; the wind teased his lips with the taste of it. Father Martin stood behind him. This was the moment that would make all the suffering worthwhile, that would give meaning to the deaths of so many.

Stephen opened his arms wide and threw his head back.

"Lord!" he cried. "Behold Your servant, Stephen. I have done as You commanded. I have brought a crusade of children to this place. Now I await Your blessing and the fulfillment of Your promise. Part this sea, O Lord, as You did for the Israelites, that we may walk through in triumph to Your Holy Land."

He opened his eyes, knowing he was about to be part of a miracle such as no one standing there could ever imagine.

Nothing happened.

A wave lapped softly on the shore.

"Lord!" Stephen cried. "Hear me!"

The waters sparkled in the now-risen sun as if mocking him.

The hum of voices resumed, then grew louder. Near him he heard a scornful laugh.

"A messenger of God, indeed," a voice sneered.

"A fool, more like," echoed another.

"You lied!" Robert clutched the pommel of his sword. His brother, Geoffrey, stood by him. Their faces were contorted with fury. Other boys crowded in behind them.

"You brought us all this way. . . . We left our homes . . . our families . . . all for naught?"

"No!" Stephen protested. His head swam; the nausea in his belly threatened to overwhelm him. "It will happen! It will!"

He turned back to the sea. Again, he cried out to God.

No answer but the raucous squawking of the sea birds that circled endlessly above them.

"A curse on you!" Robert cried. Without another word, the brothers turned and ran for their horses.

Stephen could only watch.

The townspeople, laughing and jeering, began to make their way home. A sea of children's faces turned up to Stephen. Their eyes pinned him to the spot—accusing, unbelieving. Some were sobbing. Others cried out in anger. For an instant Stephen cringed, afraid they were going to attack. Then they, too, turned their backs and began to leave. In small groups, in large groups, turning only to hurl accusations at him, they abandoned him. He was left standing alone.

Not entirely alone. Father Martin, deathly pale, stood behind him. Renard slumped upon the stones, tears streaming down his face. Angeline stood, stricken, by his side.

+ + +

The villagers did not come back. The children who sought shelter in the town were cast out. By nightfall they had returned to gather helplessly around Stephen. They waited for him to tell them what to do next, but he did not know.

Father Martin knelt in prayer at the water's edge, but Stephen could not pray with him. He felt abandoned. Betrayed. Angeline tried to talk to him, but he could not make sense of her words, could not answer. That night he sat without moving, heedless of the cold wind that swept in off the sea, heedless of the hardness of the stones upon which he sat. The murmur of the waves was a taunting reminder of his failure. By dawn he was weak with fatigue and despair.

"Try again," Renard urged as the sun rose. "Try again!"

But he would not.

CHAPTER SEVENTEEN

With the rising of the sun, Angeline came to Stephen. She sounded as if she were barely holding back panic. In his despair he had forgotten that she was even there.

"You must make a decision, Stephen," she said. "We cannot stay here, and the townspeople will not have us back. What are we to do?"

Stephen did not answer. He stared at the shining sea—his enemy now. He looked at the children crowding the beach. They were not talking, just waiting, staring at him. Except for a few priests and monks, most of the older men and women had left them to their fate. The minstrels were long gone. He turned away, sick to his heart. He could not meet their eyes, but he knew Angeline was right. He had to do something, but what? His mind still spun with the impossibility of what had happened. He couldn't think. Could not accept that God had deserted him. How had he failed? What had he done wrong? He rubbed at the scars on his left hand so hard that the skin tore and began to bleed. He did not notice that, either.

Then, in the distance, he saw the figures of two men approaching. He could do nothing but stand and wait for them, but he braced himself. He knew they would be emissaries of the count and the bishop, come to tell them to leave. He had promised to stay no more than one night and they had already stayed two. Father Martin saw them at the same instant. He rose from his knees where he had been praying and came to stand beside Stephen. When the men reached the stretch of pebbles on which he stood, however, Stephen was puzzled. These were not priests nor servants of the count. They were obviously merchants, well dressed and portly. One of them puffed, out of breath, as they came up to him.

"You are the boy, Stephen?" the other asked.

"I am," Stephen answered, tensing himself for what might be about to come. There was no pride left in his voice now.

"We have heard of your plight," the man continued. "Allow us to introduce ourselves. I am Hugo Ferrus and this is my friend and partner, William Porquierres. I believe we might be able to assist you."

"How?" Stephen spat the word out, certain that the men wished only to gloat over him. "How could you possibly help us?"

Father Martin grasped his arm. "Hear what they have to say, Stephen," he said.

"The sea did not part for you . . ." the man called Porquierres began, still panting.

"You know well it did not," Stephen snapped. "Have you come to torment me as well?"

"Then what you need are ships," Porquierres continued.

"And how are we to acquire ships?" Stephen asked, his voice bitter. "God did not answer my prayer to part the sea, do you think He will send us *ships*?"

"No, He most probably will not," Ferrus agreed, unruffled by Stephen's outburst. "But we have ships and we will make them available to you and to your followers."

"We have nothing with which to pay you," Stephen replied, his words harsh and angry now. Why had these men come to torment him further? They would want to be paid and paid well to take thousands of children to the Holy Land, and they must know that he had no means to do so. But the man's next words left him speechless.

"We require no payment," Ferrus said. "This we will do for the love and mercy of God alone."

"You would do this?" Father Martin burst out, incredulous.

Porquierres smiled at him. "We do what we can in the service of the Lord," he said. "If we can help these innocents to reach their destination, then surely it is our Christian duty to do so."

Stephen stared at him. The man's voice seemed glib and oily, but slowly his promise sank in. Could it be possible? Could this be the way? He hesitated, but Renard let out a shout of joy and ran toward the assembled children, crying the news.

"Ships!" he bellowed. "We have ships to take us to the Holy Land!"

His words spread like a wave of fire.

"You will help us?" Stephen asked. The man worried him. But what did that matter? What Porquierres was offering was salvation!

The man bowed his head, but not before Stephen caught him exchanging a quick glance and a sly smile with his partner. When he looked back at Stephen the smile was gone, and his face was arranged in a show of sincerity.

"It is our duty," he said.

Suspicion snaked into Stephen's mind, but he blocked it out. How could he question this? These were good Christian men. Surely they had been sent by God. Surely he had mis-read that smile—the tone of the man's voice. He felt the tri-umph rise within him again. It was impossible to resist! He whipped around to face the children who had come running to him.

"God has answered our prayers in His own way!" he cried. "We *will* go to the Holy Land. We *will* restore Jeru-salem to the true faith. God wills it!" His heart grew light and he went on, his voice becoming stronger and stronger with each word. "Those who have deserted us will hear of our triumph! They will hear of it and they will regret their faithlessness to their dying day. To *you* will go the honour and the glory!"

He fell to his knees to give thanks to the Lord and to beg forgiveness for his doubts. He did not notice that, although Father Martin joined him in prayer, Angeline did not. When he finally opened his eyes and looked up, it was to see her still standing, staring at Ferrus and Porquierres with an odd expression on her face. Her mouth was set and her eyes cold. He had no time for her puzzling behaviour now, though. He rose and looked beyond her to the rem-nants of his followers who had knelt to pray with him. So few now, out of the many who had followed him—probably less than a thousand. But they were the faithful. They were the ones who would reap the rewards. The scarlet crosses on their breasts and shoulders swam before his eyes like a curtain of red.

✦ ✦ ✦

The day they set sail was bright with sunshine, late in August. Only four months since he had heard his name called on that high field, Stephen thought. It seemed so much longer. Surely it was a lifetime ago, not just four short months. . . .

The sea sparkled and glinted, small waves slapped against the hull of the ship with a soothing, reassuring regularity. Father Martin and the other priests who had elected to sail with them said Mass before they embarked, beseeching God to lend them His blessing for the journey. As they cleared the harbour and the sailors raised great, cracking sails above their heads, Stephen stood with Angeline, braced against the rolling of the ship, staring eastward. He drank in the sounds and smells of the sea. It was no longer their enemy, but their accomplice. The ship sped through the waves. They would reach the Holy Land in little more than a week, Porquierres had assured him.

There were seven ships in all, filled with children and young people, a few older men and women who had straggled back, and several priests and monks. Each ship carried as many people as it could. Stephen could see four following close behind, two others sailed on his left, between his ship and the shoreline. One of them had dark red sails— Renard was on board that ship. Angeline and Father Martin had managed to stay close to Stephen in the mad dash of children clambering to board the ships that morning, but despite Stephen's efforts to hold onto him, Renard had been swept away with another group. The last Stephen had seen of him was his despairing face staring back at him, his mouth open in a cry that could not be heard over the clamour. Stephen had shouted back, reassuring him that they would be reunited at the end of their voyage, but he did not think that Renard had understood. Surely they would. They would *all* be reunited.

Thinking of Renard reminded him of Angeline's friend.

"Where is the girl, Alys?" he asked. "What will she do now that Robert and Geoffrey have deserted us?"

"She chose to stay with the woman who took care of her in Marseilles," Angeline said. "Madame LaFontaine said she had need of a girl to help her. She offered to take me as well," she added.

"Why did you not stay?" Stephen asked.

"She had no need of two girls," Angeline replied. "She was only being kind." Then, so quietly that Stephen could almost think that he imagined the words, she added, "Besides, I did not want to leave you."

This time it was she who reached for Stephen's hand.

✦ ✦ ✦

Once they were out on the open sea, a sailor ordered Stephen and Angeline below with the others. Stephen wanted to check on the children in any case, but as he climbed down the steep ladder leading to the space below decks, a fearful smell assaulted him. Already, many of the children were suffering from the rolling motion of the ship. The stink of vomit was overwhelming. He had not been feeling sick up to then, but in those close quarters his stomach began to rebel. He turned to climb back up on deck.

"I must have air," he said to Angeline.

But the sailor who had ordered them below was still there. As Stephen started to emerge, the sailor cursed at him.

"You were ordered below," he said, and slammed the hatch down in his face.

Stephen almost fell back down the ladder.

"What are you doing?" he shouted. "I wish to go back up on deck!"

"You'll stay down there," the sailor yelled back.

"For how long?" Stephen cried, furious at the insolence. Did the man not know who he was? He banged on the hatch with his fist.

"You'll stay there until the master decides otherwise," the sailor yelled. "There are far too many of you to allow you all up on deck. Stay down there and keep out of the way."

"I would speak with the master," Stephen shouted again, but this time there was no response.

Furious, Stephen turned back to the others and stumbled over to where Father Martin waited for him. Angeline had made a place for herself close by the priest.

"The master shall hear of this," he muttered, then concentrated on willing his stomach to settle.

The children were crammed together so tightly they could hardly move. Walking around was impossible, even if the ship had not been rolling so constantly. The only light came from slits high up in the hull, too far above them to see out of. It was not long until all were prostrate with sickness and the pots that had been provided to hold their bodily wastes were overflowing. Filth sloshed all around them. Angeline and Father Martin did what they could for the children, but they were as ill as all the rest. Stephen fumed, but no matter how many times he banged on the hatch and called out, no one answered.

Gradually the light faded as night took over. The darkness was impenetrable. There was no sleep for Stephen, nor for Angeline. She huddled close to him.

"I do not trust Porquierres and Ferrus," she muttered. "I think they have but sent us from one hell to another."

Exhausted, Stephen chose not to hear her.

CHAPTER EIGHTEEN

It was not until late the next day that the hatch was thrown back, letting a welcome blast of fresh air pour through. Stephen leaped to his feet and pushed his way through the mass of bodies. He had to speak to the master and make clear to him who they were and what their mission was.

"Come with me," he called to Father Martin. "He must listen to you, a priest."

"May I come, too?" Angeline asked. She was as pale as death and weak from vomiting. "I must get up into the air."

Other children dragged themselves to their feet as well, but a sailor's face appeared in the opening and yelled down to them.

"Twenty at a time. No more."

Stephen took a great gulp of air as he emerged from the stinking hold, then tottered to the rail and vomited yet again, over it, and into the sea. He held himself up weakly by the railing until he gathered strength enough to stand upright. Then he looked around for a sailor to take a message to the master. The same man who had ordered him down below the day before was standing nearby, watching the retching children with disgust. Stephen made his way over to him with as much dignity as he could muster.

"I must see the master," he announced.

The sailor laughed and turned his back on him.

"You insult our Lord himself when you insult me!" Stephen cried. "Do you not know who we are?"

"I know you are a rabble of children, that's who you are," the man replied, turning back and spitting at Stephen's feet.

"We are a crusade of the young, not a rabble," Stephen shot back. "Chosen by God himself to liberate the Holy Land and restore it to the true faith."

Weak and filthy though he was, there was power still in Stephen's voice, conviction enough in his eyes to make the man pause.

"The master is over there," he said grudgingly, and pointed to the forecastle.

"Take us to him," Stephen ordered, drawing himself up as tall as he could.

Muttering under his breath, the man motioned for Stephen to follow him.

"Which one is the master?" Father Martin asked.

It was only then that Stephen noticed another man standing half hidden by a stack of roped-down barrels.

His question was answered as one man turned toward them and the other took a step back, almost as if to conceal himself in the shadows.

"What is it you wish?" the master boomed out. "Why are you bothering me?"

"We must speak with you," Stephen replied, making his way up to him and trying to match his steps to the roll and pitch of the ship. He staggered and reached for the railing to steady himself.

"You will be fed when we have the time," the master roared. "Go back where you belong."

"It is not for food that I have come," Stephen answered.

"Although that will be very welcome," Father Martin put in hastily.

"It is to take you to task for the way we are being treated," Stephen said. "Do you not know who we are?" he repeated.

"I know that you are scum that I am being forced to transport," the master spat out.

At that the man in the shadows spoke out.

"And for which you are being well paid," he said curtly. "Enough!" Then he glared at Stephen.

"Go back," he ordered. "We know who you are and why you are here. You will be taken care of, never fear."

The exchange between the two men sent a chill up Stephen's back. There was something not right here. Angeline's words echoed in his mind.

Father Martin must have felt something of the same unease.

"We are doing God's will," he said to the master. "Take care how you deal with us."

"You will be dealt with exactly as you deserve," the stranger replied, then he retreated into the enclosed cabin behind him.

"Who is that man?" Father Martin demanded, looking after him with a frown.

"He is the agent of Hugo Ferrus and William Porquierres," the master replied. "And not a man to be trifled with. Now you have had your assurances, get back to your followers. There is bad weather approaching and if you wish to be fed, it will have to be done quickly."

Before they were given food, however, all who were up on deck were herded back down into the hold.

"I do not think I can stand it," Angeline said as she climbed down the ladder. The smell smote them like a wall.

Later that evening, buckets were lowered with maggoty salt meat and a kind of gruel, all slopped together. It was not fit for pigs, but most of the children were too sick to eat it anyway.

✦ ✦ ✦

That night the wind rose. The waves began to slam against the sides of the ship with alarming intensity. Stephen had thought the rolling to be bad before, but now the ship wallowed and pitched from side to side with such force, that even crushed in together as they were, they found themselves thrown around. Angeline crawled away from Stephen and Father Martin to see if there was anything she could do for the children, who wailed in terror. It was not long until she crawled back.

"Two of the little ones have died," she gasped. "Help me with them."

Father Martin and Stephen followed her to the other end of the hold. They made their way with difficulty through, around, and over the other children. Most of them were so distressed they did not even notice they were being trodden upon. The priest blessed the dead children, but there was nothing else he could do.

All that night and all the next day they suffered in the hold. Stephen began to think that Angeline had spoken more truly than she had known when she called that place a hell.

By the time the storm finally ceased, they were all too weak to move. Three more children had died. When the hatch was raised it took a while before anyone could react. Father Martin was the first to collect himself.

"We must get up on deck," he said, "and take as many of the children as we can."

A sailor's face appeared at the opening, grimacing at the stink that rose to greet him.

"There are dead children down here," Father Martin called up. "You must send someone down to take them up."

"Take them up yourselves," came the reply. The face disappeared.

Stephen dragged himself to his feet and picked up one of the small bodies. Angeline and Father Martin staggered to their feet to help him. Between them, they carried all the dead children up to the deck. Father Martin stepped forward to give them a final blessing, but before he could do so, a sailor picked them up and flung them, one by one, over the rail. Angeline cried out, Father Martin made the sign of the cross, but there was nothing more to be done.

Then, as Stephen looked around him, he realized he could count only five ships. The two that had sailed to the landward side of them were missing.

"Those two ships—the one with the red sails and the other one—where are they?" he asked the nearest sailor.

"Foundered on the rocks of San Pietro in the storm, they did," he answered. "Every soul aboard them perished. And it was only by the grace of God that we did not follow them."

The grace of God? Stephen looked at the children dragging themselves out of the hold into the fresh air. How many had died on those two ships? And how many more would die before they reached Jerusalem?

Then he remembered—Renard had been on the ship with the red sails. Weak and annoying as he had been, Renard had stayed faithful to him for the whole journey. He had stood by Stephen even when the sea did not part, and so many others had abandoned him. Renard had been one of the first four boys to believe in him and follow him. And now he was the last of them to die.

He had lost them all. Betrayed them all.

He dropped his head onto the railing and wept.

✦ ✦ ✦

Father Martin did his best to console Stephen.

"They are with God," he said. "Their journey is over."

His words were meant to be comforting, Stephen knew, but the priest's face was so stricken and the pain behind the words so deep, that Stephen could feel no solace.

That night he stood at the prow of the ship, watching the waves break on either side of them in foam and spumes of white water that glistened in the light of the new-risen moon. Then he became aware of Angeline at his side. She stood in silence for a long time. Finally, she spoke.

"I am sorry for the things I've said, Stephen," she said. "For my lack of faith. You chastised me for it, and you were right. But *you* cannot lose faith now. *You* cannot despair." The wind clawed at her words, fragmented them into the salt-heavy air. "We need you. If you fail us, we are doomed and all this will have been for naught!"

Her words seemed to tear a rent in his soul.

"Is it worth it?" he cried. "So many deaths! Is it worth it?"

"You have to believe that it is."

"I have to. But can I?" Stephen raised his face to the wind. He felt the spray, cold and stinging on his cheeks.

"It is too much," he whispered. "It is too much to ask of me."

"But it *was* asked." It was almost a sob, thrown into the dark of the night. "It *was* asked of you—and you accepted."

In his heart he knew she spoke the truth. He had accepted the responsibility. He had exulted in his power, had gloried in the belief that God had chosen him. Him! A simple shepherd boy. To what unimagined heights had he been raised!

But if he had known the cost. . . ?

✦ ✦ ✦

The next few days were brilliant and sun-filled; the remaining ships sped through the waves. The children were allowed up on deck in small groups and Angeline organized some of the older youths into helping her clean up below decks as much as possible. Father Martin hiked his robes up to his knees and helped as well. The food was still foul, however. It was a way for Stephen to vent his bitterness, and it was only with difficulty that Father Martin restrained him from demanding to see the master again and voicing his complaints.

"Be patient, Stephen," the priest said. "It matters not. What is important is that we are speeding toward Jerusalem. Toward the Holy Land. Feed your spirit, worry not about your belly."

The children, recovered from their sea sickness, were bright and cheerful. No more died. Some even began to get a blush in their cheeks from the wind and the sun, and their eyes sparkled. Once again, they sang and the ship sped on accompanied by the sound of hymns. Each morning Father Martin said Mass, each evening Stephen preached, but no matter how hard he tried, no matter how much he prayed and implored God's mercy, it was impossible to summon up the fire and the energy that had filled him before. He felt hollow. Empty. He made his confession to Father Martin, but even the priest's absolution did not take away his doubts. He scanned the horizon each day, searching for the first sight of land. Then one morning there was a different smell to the air when he went up on deck, Angeline close at his heels.

"It is land, Stephen," Angeline said. "I know it!"

By midday they could see a low, rolling outline against the horizon which revealed itself to be seemingly endless dunes of sand. Fringed-leaf trees such as the ones they had

166

seen on the beach at Marseilles lined the shore. Two tall spires rose up behind the trees like sentinels, reaching up to the implacable sun that beat down mercilessly. The wind that ushered them in was hot. Sea birds began to fly over, almost as if they were escorting the ships to shore. Children crowded the rails, pointing and shouting.

"The Holy Land!" Stephen whispered.

Finally. It was over.

They sailed past the ruins of a great lighthouse into a wide, calm harbour. Together, Stephen and Angeline watched as the ship was made fast to a wharf. A throng of turbaned and brightly robed men waited there. The sailors threw out lines to them. A plank was laid against the side.

Stephen bowed his head in prayer, then lifted his chin and tossed his hair out of his eyes.

God had delivered them here. His faith had been rewarded.

Now. Now it was up to him.

He did not see Father Martin gazing at the lighthouse with a furrowed brow.

"I have heard of such a wondrous lighthouse," the priest murmured, "but not in the Holy Land. The pharos I have read of stands in the harbour of Alexandria. In Egypt. The land of the heathens."

Stephen paid no heed to the words. His eyes were fixed on the waves of sand as if he could will Jerusalem to rise up out of the shimmering desert heat.

Nor did he notice as the men began to swarm up the side of the ship.

HISTORICAL NOTE

The boy named Stephen of Cloyes really did exist. According to recorded history, in April of the year 1212, a man did appear to him as he was tending his sheep and gave him a letter commanding him to lead an army of children to liberate Jerusalem. We have no way of knowing who this man was, but Stephen was convinced that he was the Christ and the letter was from God. His Children's Crusade, as it came to be known, marched across France to the port of Marseilles and was at one time about twenty thousand strong.

After his arduous journey, Stephen and the remnants of his followers set sail from Marseilles in late August and were not heard of again for eighteen years. At that time, a priest who had been one of Stephen's followers returned from Egypt and solved the mystery of their disappearance. He told of how only two days out of Marseilles, a storm had arisen and two of the ships sank. The remaining ships did not take the children to the Holy Land. Instead, Porquierres and Ferrus had made arrangements to sell the children as slaves in Bougie, on the coast of northern Africa, in Egypt, and in the Holy Land.

This priest also recounted, however, that many of those in the crusade who were literate and who were sold as slaves in Egypt, had made good lives for themselves. Muslims treated their slaves well. It was an act of faith for a Muslim to free a slave. As well, the sultan at the time, al-Adil, was anxious for his princes and nobles to learn the western languages and he used these literate children and priests as teachers and tutors. But of Stephen himself, nothing further is known after he set sail from Marseilles. Nor is anything known about the fate of the letter.

The Scarlet Cross is the story of Stephen and his crusade based on the historical facts as we know them.

In *Angeline*, I have taken the liberty of imagining how this story might have continued.

Karleen Bradford
2006

ACKNOWLEDGEMENTS

I would like, yet again, to thank my good friends Jan Andrews and Rachna Gilmore for their patience, honesty, and expertise. They read far too many drafts of this novel. And to my husband, Jim, my thanks for helping me find the ending.

To my editor, Lynne Missen, and agent, Marie Campbell, I extend my gratitude for their vision. It was they who saw the pattern that this book and its sequel, *Angeline*, should take. And thank you, Noelle Zitzer, for shepherding it through its final stages.

Thank you to Kathryn Cole for her careful editing, and to Lynn and David Bennett of the Transatlantic Literary Agency for their support and continued guidance.

My gratitude, also, to the Canada Council for the grant that made the research for this book possible.

The adventure continues. . .

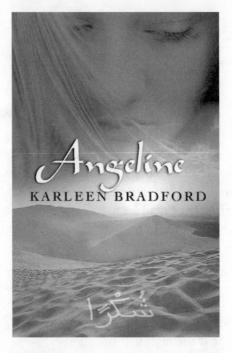

Don't miss *Angeline*.

ISBN-13: 978-0-00-639344-3
ISBN-10: 0-00-639344-6
$7.99